JUST ME

(A Cami Lark Mystery —Book One)

BLAKE PIERCE

Blake Pierce

Blake Pierce is the USA Today bestselling author of the RILEY PAGE mystery series, which includes seventeen books. Blake Pierce is also the author of the MACKENZIE WHITE mystery series, comprising fourteen books; of the AVERY BLACK mystery series, comprising six books; of the KERI LOCKE mystery series, comprising five books; of the MAKING OF RILEY PAIGE mystery series, comprising six books; of the KATE WISE mystery series, comprising seven books; of the CHLOE FINE psychological suspense mystery, comprising six books; of the JESSIE HUNT psychological suspense thriller series, comprising twenty six books; of the AU PAIR psychological suspense thriller series, comprising three books; of the ZOE PRIME mystery series, comprising six books; of the ADELE SHARP mystery series, comprising sixteen books, of the EUROPEAN VOYAGE cozy mystery series, comprising six books; of the LAURA FROST FBI suspense thriller, comprising eleven books; of the ELLA DARK FBI suspense thriller, comprising fourteen books (and counting); of the A YEAR IN EUROPE cozy mystery series, comprising nine books, of the AVA GOLD mystery series, comprising six books (and counting); of the RACHEL GIFT mystery series, comprising ten books (and counting); of the VALERIE LAW mystery series, comprising nine books (and counting); of the PAIGE KING mystery series, comprising eight books (and counting); of the MAY MOORE mystery series, comprising eleven books (and counting); the CORA SHIELDS mystery series, comprising five books (and counting); of the NICKY LYONS mystery series, comprising five books (and counting), and of the new CAMI LARK mystery series, comprising five books (and counting).

An avid reader and lifelong fan of the mystery and thriller genres, Blake loves to hear from you, so please feel free to visit www.blakepierceauthor.com to learn more and stay in touch.

ISBN: 978-1-0943-8026-1

BOOKS BY BLAKE PIERCE

CAMI LARK MYSTERY SERIES
JUST ME (Book #1)
JUST OUTSIDE (Book #2)
JUST RIGHT (Book #3)
JUST FORGET (Book #4)
JUST ONCE (Book #5)

NICKY LYONS MYSTERY SERIES
ALL MINE (Book #1)
ALL HIS (Book #2)
ALL HE SEES (Book #3)
ALL ALONE (Book #4)
ALL FOR ONE (Book #5)

CORA SHIELDS MYSTERY SERIES
UNDONE (Book #1)
UNWANTED (Book #2)
UNHINGED (Book #3)
UNSAID (Book #4)
UNGLUED (Book #5)

MAY MOORE SUSPENSE THRILLER
NEVER RUN (Book #1)
NEVER TELL (Book #2)
NEVER LIVE (Book #3)
NEVER HIDE (Book #4)
NEVER FORGIVE (Book #5)
NEVER AGAIN (Book #6)
NEVER LOOK BACK (Book #7)
NEVER FORGET (Book #8)
NEVER LET GO (Book #9)
NEVER PRETEND (Book #10)
NEVER HESITATE (Book #11)

PAIGE KING MYSTERY SERIES
THE GIRL HE PINED (Book #1)
THE GIRL HE CHOSE (Book #2)

THE GIRL HE TOOK (Book #3)
THE GIRL HE WISHED (Book #4)
THE GIRL HE CROWNED (Book #5)
THE GIRL HE WATCHED (Book #6)
THE GIRL HE WANTED (Book #7)
THE GIRL HE CLAIMED (Book #8)

VALERIE LAW MYSTERY SERIES
NO MERCY (Book #1)
NO PITY (Book #2)
NO FEAR (Book #3)
NO SLEEP (Book #4)
NO QUARTER (Book #5)
NO CHANCE (Book #6)
NO REFUGE (Book #7)
NO GRACE (Book #8)
NO ESCAPE (Book #9)

RACHEL GIFT MYSTERY SERIES
HER LAST WISH (Book #1)
HER LAST CHANCE (Book #2)
HER LAST HOPE (Book #3)
HER LAST FEAR (Book #4)
HER LAST CHOICE (Book #5)
HER LAST BREATH (Book #6)
HER LAST MISTAKE (Book #7)
HER LAST DESIRE (Book #8)
HER LAST REGRET (Book #9)
HER LAST HOUR (Book #10)

AVA GOLD MYSTERY SERIES
CITY OF PREY (Book #1)
CITY OF FEAR (Book #2)
CITY OF BONES (Book #3)
CITY OF GHOSTS (Book #4)
CITY OF DEATH (Book #5)
CITY OF VICE (Book #6)

A YEAR IN EUROPE
A MURDER IN PARIS (Book #1)
DEATH IN FLORENCE (Book #2)

VENGEANCE IN VIENNA (Book #3)
A FATALITY IN SPAIN (Book #4)

ELLA DARK FBI SUSPENSE THRILLER
GIRL, ALONE (Book #1)
GIRL, TAKEN (Book #2)
GIRL, HUNTED (Book #3)
GIRL, SILENCED (Book #4)
GIRL, VANISHED (Book 5)
GIRL ERASED (Book #6)
GIRL, FORSAKEN (Book #7)
GIRL, TRAPPED (Book #8)
GIRL, EXPENDABLE (Book #9)
GIRL, ESCAPED (Book #10)
GIRL, HIS (Book #11)
GIRL, LURED (Book #12)
GIRL, MISSING (Book #13)
GIRL, UNKNOWN (Book #14)

LAURA FROST FBI SUSPENSE THRILLER
ALREADY GONE (Book #1)
ALREADY SEEN (Book #2)
ALREADY TRAPPED (Book #3)
ALREADY MISSING (Book #4)
ALREADY DEAD (Book #5)
ALREADY TAKEN (Book #6)
ALREADY CHOSEN (Book #7)
ALREADY LOST (Book #8)
ALREADY HIS (Book #9)
ALREADY LURED (Book #10)
ALREADY COLD (Book #11)

EUROPEAN VOYAGE COZY MYSTERY SERIES
MURDER (AND BAKLAVA) (Book #1)
DEATH (AND APPLE STRUDEL) (Book #2)
CRIME (AND LAGER) (Book #3)
MISFORTUNE (AND GOUDA) (Book #4)
CALAMITY (AND A DANISH) (Book #5)
MAYHEM (AND HERRING) (Book #6)

ADELE SHARP MYSTERY SERIES

LEFT TO DIE (Book #1)
LEFT TO RUN (Book #2)
LEFT TO HIDE (Book #3)
LEFT TO KILL (Book #4)
LEFT TO MURDER (Book #5)
LEFT TO ENVY (Book #6)
LEFT TO LAPSE (Book #7)
LEFT TO VANISH (Book #8)
LEFT TO HUNT (Book #9)
LEFT TO FEAR (Book #10)
LEFT TO PREY (Book #11)
LEFT TO LURE (Book #12)
LEFT TO CRAVE (Book #13)
LEFT TO LOATHE (Book #14)
LEFT TO HARM (Book #15)
LEFT TO RUIN (Book #16)

THE AU PAIR SERIES
ALMOST GONE (Book#1)
ALMOST LOST (Book #2)
ALMOST DEAD (Book #3)

ZOE PRIME MYSTERY SERIES
FACE OF DEATH (Book#1)
FACE OF MURDER (Book #2)
FACE OF FEAR (Book #3)
FACE OF MADNESS (Book #4)
FACE OF FURY (Book #5)
FACE OF DARKNESS (Book #6)

A JESSIE HUNT PSYCHOLOGICAL SUSPENSE SERIES
THE PERFECT WIFE (Book #1)
THE PERFECT BLOCK (Book #2)
THE PERFECT HOUSE (Book #3)
THE PERFECT SMILE (Book #4)
THE PERFECT LIE (Book #5)
THE PERFECT LOOK (Book #6)
THE PERFECT AFFAIR (Book #7)
THE PERFECT ALIBI (Book #8)
THE PERFECT NEIGHBOR (Book #9)
THE PERFECT DISGUISE (Book #10)

THE PERFECT SECRET (Book #11)
THE PERFECT FAÇADE (Book #12)
THE PERFECT IMPRESSION (Book #13)
THE PERFECT DECEIT (Book #14)
THE PERFECT MISTRESS (Book #15)
THE PERFECT IMAGE (Book #16)
THE PERFECT VEIL (Book #17)
THE PERFECT INDISCRETION (Book #18)
THE PERFECT RUMOR (Book #19)
THE PERFECT COUPLE (Book #20)
THE PERFECT MURDER (Book #21)
THE PERFECT HUSBAND (Book #22)
THE PERFECT SCANDAL (Book #23)
THE PERFECT MASK (Book #24)
THE PERFECT RUSE (Book #25)
THE PERFECT VENEER (Book #26)

CHLOE FINE PSYCHOLOGICAL SUSPENSE SERIES

NEXT DOOR (Book #1)
A NEIGHBOR'S LIE (Book #2)
CUL DE SAC (Book #3)
SILENT NEIGHBOR (Book #4)
HOMECOMING (Book #5)
TINTED WINDOWS (Book #6)

KATE WISE MYSTERY SERIES

IF SHE KNEW (Book #1)
IF SHE SAW (Book #2)
IF SHE RAN (Book #3)
IF SHE HID (Book #4)
IF SHE FLED (Book #5)
IF SHE FEARED (Book #6)
IF SHE HEARD (Book #7)

THE MAKING OF RILEY PAIGE SERIES

WATCHING (Book #1)
WAITING (Book #2)
LURING (Book #3)
TAKING (Book #4)
STALKING (Book #5)
KILLING (Book #6)

RILEY PAIGE MYSTERY SERIES
ONCE GONE (Book #1)
ONCE TAKEN (Book #2)
ONCE CRAVED (Book #3)
ONCE LURED (Book #4)
ONCE HUNTED (Book #5)
ONCE PINED (Book #6)
ONCE FORSAKEN (Book #7)
ONCE COLD (Book #8)
ONCE STALKED (Book #9)
ONCE LOST (Book #10)
ONCE BURIED (Book #11)
ONCE BOUND (Book #12)
ONCE TRAPPED (Book #13)
ONCE DORMANT (Book #14)
ONCE SHUNNED (Book #15)
ONCE MISSED (Book #16)
ONCE CHOSEN (Book #17)

MACKENZIE WHITE MYSTERY SERIES
BEFORE HE KILLS (Book #1)
BEFORE HE SEES (Book #2)
BEFORE HE COVETS (Book #3)
BEFORE HE TAKES (Book #4)
BEFORE HE NEEDS (Book #5)
BEFORE HE FEELS (Book #6)
BEFORE HE SINS (Book #7)
BEFORE HE HUNTS (Book #8)
BEFORE HE PREYS (Book #9)
BEFORE HE LONGS (Book #10)
BEFORE HE LAPSES (Book #11)
BEFORE HE ENVIES (Book #12)
BEFORE HE STALKS (Book #13)
BEFORE HE HARMS (Book #14)

AVERY BLACK MYSTERY SERIES
CAUSE TO KILL (Book #1)
CAUSE TO RUN (Book #2)
CAUSE TO HIDE (Book #3)
CAUSE TO FEAR (Book #4)

CAUSE TO SAVE (Book #5)
CAUSE TO DREAD (Book #6)

KERI LOCKE MYSTERY SERIES
A TRACE OF DEATH (Book #1)
A TRACE OF MURDER (Book #2)
A TRACE OF VICE (Book #3)
A TRACE OF CRIME (Book #4)
A TRACE OF HOPE (Book #5)

PROLOGUE

"Strangulation, again?"

FBI agent Drew Connor stared at the scene in front of him, taking in the setting and circumstances of this disturbing crime—the second of its kind in two days. Everything about it, to him, was screaming "serial."

"Could be a coincidence," the other agent, Jerry Brink, argued firmly.

Connor shook his head as he looked at the body, on the slick dark tiles, between the couch and the office chair.

The study in the luxurious house was as sleek and modern as a spaceship: Chrome counters and desks, two giant screens, and charcoal leather furniture—two office chairs and a sleek couch.

It was still and quiet apart from a few pinpoint lights on the monitors. Through the large window, the well-tended backyard was peaceful and quiet. Only the occasional swish of a car broke the silence from the street beyond.

This quiet, leafy suburb of Boston was an unlikely place for a murder scene. It was Connor's home city, although he hadn't been back for more than a decade. He'd been working as an FBI Behavioral Analysis Unit specialist in Virginia. Now, thanks to a staff reshuffle and the shocking resignations of three top Boston agents, he'd been rushed back here to handle the case load. His plane had landed an hour ago, and he'd sped straight to this murder scene.

The victim was a woman, in her twenties, lying face up. Her blond hair was fanned out around her, looking pale against the flooring. She was wearing dark jeans, a gray designer top, and black trainers. Her eyes were wide, and a starburst of blood in one of them pointed the way to the cause of death, which the marks on her slender neck confirmed.

"It's the same MO. I'm telling you," he said to Brink.

Shaking his head, Brink responded, "There aren't enough similarities to be sure."

"Both young women? Both with AI goggles lying nearby?" Connor pressed his point home, frowning down at the shocking scene. "And both with that weird little picture beside the headsets?"

Behind the body, near the white virtual reality headset on the floor, lay a small, crumpled scrap of paper, a printed, postage-stamp picture of what looked like an AI figure. This one was dark-haired with wide, green eyes. Connor recalled that the other had been blond and blue-eyed.

"Everyone's online these days," Brink insisted in a low voice. "Those pictures could be collectibles or used in a game, or even come with the headsets. You'd better think carefully before you say that there's a serial killer at work. A week before Patriots' Day and the Boston Marathon? I can tell you already what the state governor will think about that. He'll rip Fraser a new one."

Connor nodded grimly at the mention of Fraser, their boss. Pressing his lips together, he raised a hand to his temples to ease a throbbing headache. He caught sight of himself in the narrow strip of mirror near the door, noticing the lines in his tanned face and the threads of gray in his short, dark hair. His face was showing the strain of his job, which was stressful and demanding, and as of this morning, felt a hundred times more so.

"She was online. Most probably, gaming. And wearing that headset. How else would a killer have managed to get so close, with barely any sign of a struggle?" Connor persisted. At the last scene, there had been no more than minor scuffing on the floor and a few flecks of woolen fabric under the victim's fingernails, an indication that the killer had worn gloves as he'd wrapped his hands around her neck.

To Connor, it was obvious that these women had been immersed in the sights and sounds of the virtual world. What they had been doing was not yet clear. Police at the first scene had said that all machines and devices were turned off. That must have been done after death.

And it looked to be the same here. Hence the utter silence of this room and the blankness of the screens.

They weren't going to get a whole lot of information out of anything here. Connor knew that to find out where these victims had been interacting, to trace their digital footprints, to find out the common links that joined them to each other, and presumably to the killer, would require specialist knowledge of the virtual world.

The resignation of the three bright young agents who specialized in tech had been a huge blow to the Boston office. They'd been lured away to work for a well-funded tech startup, leaving a skills gap that would be difficult to fill at short notice. Their cybercrime team was now spread thin.

Connor didn't have IT knowledge, but he had decades of experience in crime investigation, probably double what the more junior Jerry had. And he was utterly sure that this was the start of a serial. The signatures, the placement of the victims, and the feel of the scenes all pointed to it.

They had been killed while online. That was how he'd gotten so close, so easily. And taking that logic further, together with the small, crumpled signature the killer had left, he wondered if these women had somehow been targeted or tracked while online.

Connor stared at the pale gray walls of the study and glanced down at the virtual reality headset.

Never before had he, personally, felt so helpless in the face of a serial killer.

One thing he knew for sure: unless they got a lead on this, and fast, this shadowy killer, familiar with worlds he knew nothing about, would be way ahead of them.

CHAPTER ONE

Sitting in the cramped upstairs room that was a converted piercing and tattoo salon, Cami Lark seethed with anger as she listened to the artist who was doing her piercing.

"That's not fair," Cami said as Bella turned to the equipment on her tray, soaking a cotton swab with disinfectant. "Nobody should treat another person that way and abuse their authority like that."

Cami pushed her hair back so that Bella could pin it, holding the locks that were dyed pitch black from her natural blond. She wore a daring style that was shaved on one side and shoulder length on the other. Her brows were tinted dark, which brought out her green, intense eyes.

"Mom thought the job was going to be great," Bella continued. "And I was so proud of her for getting it."

"When did it all go wrong?" Cami asked. Last time she'd been here, two months ago, Bella had been thrilled about her mom's new job.

"There was a team reshuffle the week after she joined, and a new manager was brought in from another department. Tony's now her immediate senior. And he's bullying her nonstop, criticizing her, pulling her work apart. Despite the fact she's highly qualified for the job and the hardest worker. She's the only woman on the team, and he's not picking on any of the men that way."

Cami thought that was so wrong. What right did that toxic boss have to bully a woman at work just because he was a chauvinistic brute, who wanted to impose his beliefs on her and misuse his power?

At twenty-one, Cami knew she wanted to live in a better world than what was out there. And if it wasn't, then she needed to make it that way. Nothing else but her own efforts would change things, right? That was how things got done: by people being brave enough to make themselves heard and stand up to those who were abusing their authority.

"He's making her life a misery," Bella agreed sadly. "She dreads going to work every day."

"We need to do something about that," Cami insisted. Reminded of the way her own overbearing father had treated her, she seethed all over again.

Immediately, she saw the flare of panic in Bella's eyes.

"No, no!" Bella said. "Don't you even think about it, don't you dare do anything."

"Why?" Cami asked innocently, but her mind was already racing.

"Girl, you have a couple of months to go 'till graduation. Don't sabotage your future. You could lose more than your scholarship if this guy finds out you've been hacking into his personal messages, or his bank account, or wherever else you try to cause him damage. I know you! You want to set the world right, and that all seems well and good, but that's not how things work."

"What's his last name?" Cami asked.

"I'm not telling you!" Bella looked really angry.

"You don't need to worry. It won't come back to your mom."

"It's you I'm worried about. Put that phone away. Now! And hold still."

Reluctantly, Cami complied, but she hadn't given up on the idea. The same compulsion that she felt in her classes at MIT, where she was the star IT student in her final semester, overtook her now.

IT ability could be used to change the world, and Cami wanted to change things. She wanted to upturn what wasn't working and balance out what was. But at this moment, more than anything, she wanted to cause this toxic man some grief, just for payback for Bella's mother. She had his first name and knew his role in the company. That was enough information to find him, and she resolved that she was going to.

She was sure she could find his personal cell number. That would be first prize. If she could get into the device, she could cause havoc. She could upset his life, more than he'd like. She might even find content that could compromise him. He might be a middle-level manager, but he worked for a big corporation. People who were toxic to others, in her experience, often had sins of their own to hide. Maybe if he was exposed for something unacceptable, the company would fire him. Imagine if she could get him fired?

Phones were trickier to hack than computers. So, if she couldn't access the phone, then his email would have to do. But a while ago, Cami had written her own program that often got around the phone's access issue. This would be a good chance to test it out. As her mind ran ahead on the logical path she could follow to get this payback under way, she barely noticed Bella completing her piercing.

"There you go. Done. And stay out of trouble, you hear me?"

Cami glanced up. The new earring, alongside the other two, looked like it completed a set: the two silver rings and the new white-gold stud, which looked striking and different.

"It looks great!" Cami felt happy as she handed over the cash. She loved this look.

She preferred her identity this way. Dark hair, dark brows, and dark lashes, matching the dark tattoo of a rose on her left arm. And shiny studs and rings, more piercings than what society considered the norm, bright and eye-catching like the metal details on her leather jacket.

From downstairs, she heard the tramp of footsteps coming up. Bella must have another customer, so she needed to make herself scarce, go back to her student digs, and carry on working to access his phone and get some payback for Bella's mother.

But then, she clocked that Bella was looking in a surprised way at the door, as if she hadn't expected anyone to come in after her.

Two people, as Cami now heard from the footsteps.

The door swung open and the two walked in. As Cami saw them, she realized to her shock that they were law enforcement.

Blue jackets, yellow logos. Not just law enforcement. Not just police. They were the FBI.

The FBI was here? Cami felt incredulous as she took them in. Immediately, she felt her stomach clench as she remembered what she'd done a couple of days ago.

Surely, they couldn't be here for that.

Or could they?

A solidly built man led the way. He had a lined face, threads of gray in his crisp, dark hair, and that blank, officious face that Cami associated with cops. Behind him was a younger man, with sandy-brown hair, maybe ten years younger, but the same facial expression. Those same eyes.

These weren't just cops. They were all the way up on the ladder. If they were here, this was serious business.

Bella had taken a step back toward the tiny window and was standing seemingly frozen in shock as the agents made their way unerringly over to Cami.

And then, the man in front spoke, looking at her. His voice was harsh. "FBI Special Agent Connor. Are you Ms. Cami Lark?"

This was it. Her actions from the weekend were coming back to bite her, big time.

Cami stared into his hazel eyes. Despite the instinctive churning of her stomach, she wasn't going to show any guilt about her actions. Not to this man. And she wasn't going to apologize for what she'd done. Not when there had been reasons behind it.

"That's me," she said, raising her head and staring defiantly at him.

It gave Cami a moment of satisfaction to see how taken aback this FBI agent looked by her bold admission. Then she saw his eyes narrow as he took in Cami's inky hair, her dramatic fade, her tattoo, and her studded jacket.

"It's a kid. A college kid," he muttered to his partner.

Then, to her, "You're wanted for questioning. You need to come with us to the offices."

"The offices?" Cami repeated incredulously.

"The FBI offices in Chelsea. Please accompany us downstairs now, Ms. Lark."

She heard Bella gasp in horror but didn't turn in her direction. Immediately, she knew that she was the one who'd attracted trouble to this little shop, and she was the one who'd have to deal with it. Bella didn't deserve to be caught up in this.

"You're taking me for questioning? You can't be serious!" she shot back at the agent, seeing his frown deepen.

"I don't have time to waste. Come on," he pressured her.

"This is ridiculous. Aren't there real criminals out there? You say you don't have time to waste? Isn't this exactly what you're doing now?" Cami stood her ground.

But Connor folded his arms. "Right now, we're just talking. But if you don't come with me, I will arrest you and your friend, and we'll have this same conversation with you both in handcuffs."

She heard Bella's indrawn, terrified breath and felt furious that this man was threatening her friend.

"She's got nothing to do with this. Leave her alone. I'll come with you," she said, seeing that this was now the only way to stop Bella from getting caught up in this debacle.

She headed for the door, seeing that Special Agent Connor was casting another disapproving glance at her chunky Doc Marten boots. It seemed that her entire ensemble was triggering this heavy-featured man's ire.

Cami noted how the two agents effectively bracketed her, one walking ahead and one behind, as they all clumped down the wooden treads. In fact, Connor was practically breathing down the back of her neck.

At the bottom of the stairs, a sleek gray car was waiting.

"Inside," Connor said sharply, opening the back door and indicating for her to climb inside.

Cami hesitated, wondering if she should refuse on principle. But the agent was ready, with a hand on her shoulder, pushing her down.

"Now."

Cami felt her world spinning as she was shoved into the backseat of the car, realizing that whatever she had done, this time she had gone too far—and that her world would never be the same again.

CHAPTER TWO

Cami had driven past the FBI Boston headquarters on Beech Street, Chelsea, many times. But until now, she'd barely taken notice of the tall, glass-fronted building behind its black palisade, with its black-on-white signage.

The couple of times she had noticed, she'd glanced scornfully at it, because they were law enforcement. Glorified police, nothing more.

She had no love for law enforcement. She despised them. When she'd needed them in her own life, they hadn't been able to help. Six years ago, when her older sister, Jenna, had disappeared, they'd been unable to help. The police had gotten nowhere, despite the fact that her dad, who was a local cop, had been on the team. Cami thought he hadn't tried very hard; he had assumed the rebellious Jenna was a runaway.

The FBI hadn't gotten results, even though Cami, fifteen years old at the time, had tried to call them herself and plead with them.

Law enforcement had let her family down, and she didn't want to think back on that time of sadness and loss. She'd never forgiven her dad, or any of them, for failing her and Jenna.

Now, six years too late, the FBI was suddenly taking an interest in her, that was for sure.

She was actually heading through the main gate and into the parking outside the building, trapped in the back seat of the gray Ford that was being driven by the other agent. In the passenger seat, Connor kept glancing back at her as if to make sure she was still there and hadn't vaporized herself along the way.

Cami hadn't vaporized. She glowered at him every time he looked. She was pretty sure, in fact certain, that the locks on the back doors couldn't be opened from inside. That was a no-brainer, she guessed. So, when the car stopped in the parking, she didn't even bother to touch the door handle.

She just sat and waited, and after a moment, Connor got out, walked around, and pulled the door open. He looked slightly disappointed, as if he'd been anticipating Cami would struggle with the door.

She climbed out and walked with the agents to the building's front entrance.

"Bringing in a suspect," Connor muttered to the guard, who looked at her like she was a criminal.

"Put your purse, your phone, and any other personal items in the tray," he snapped at her.

Cami complied. Then she stepped through the metal detector. A siren shriek filled the air.

"Ma'am, remove your shoes."

She stared at him. "Remove my Docs?"

"Yes, ma'am. They're triggering the metal detector."

"But they have steel toecaps. Isn't that obvious? Of course they'll trigger it. I don't have any weapons on me! Can't you tell?" she asked angrily. They took ages to lace up and unlace. These people were seriously standing here, staring at her boots, instead of being out catching real criminals.

"Remove your shoes, ma'am."

Cami sighed. Bureaucracy at its finest. She bent down and unlaced the Docs, passing them to him. He ran them through the X-ray machine, and she stepped through the metal detector in her socks.

Then the agents stood and waited impatiently, as if their systems hadn't been the issue causing this delay, as she got her shoes on and did them up again.

"Come this way," Connor said. He strode across the lobby, heading for the elevators, while the other agent walked in step with Cami.

They rode up to the fourth floor, and then headed along a tiled corridor to an office near the end. Only it wasn't an office, Cami saw when she walked in, feeling surprised and a little intimidated. This was more like an interrogation room.

There was a desk in the small room's center: one chair stood on the far side, two chairs on the near side. There was no window, only the hiss of aircon through the vents.

The pale gray walls were blank apart from a couple of laminated official notices in small print.

"Sit," Connor told her.

Cami walked around the table and sat. Her mind was accelerating ahead, fueled by a surge of adrenaline. She felt firmly on the back foot, which wasn't a familiar or a comfortable place to be. She couldn't take action. She didn't even have her phone with her. It was still in the tray, which was on the shelf behind Connor.

They'd disarmed her, taken away her weapon. Now all she had to face them with was herself.

The two agents sat down opposite her.

Cami waited to hear what they said, while at the same time, going through strategies in her head. She really hadn't thought what she'd done was traceable. That was the whole point of hacking, right?

But on the other hand, they were here, angrily checking her out. They'd tracked her to her hairdresser's and knew her by name. So somewhere along the line, she'd messed up. She thought back, trying to pinpoint where it had been.

"You know why you're here." Connor leaned his elbows on the desk and stared at her threateningly. Cami could see the lines etched on either side of his mouth. It didn't look like he smiled a lot.

"Tell me," she said, doing her best to sound noncommittal, despite the fact that she was starting to feel a little overwhelmed.

"You hacked the FBI's website. You put up a list of unsolved cases, with the message that the Bureau was useless, and changed the director's photo to a cat face."

Connor looked at Cami, and now his expression said he was three moves ahead. He was waiting for Cami to deny this statement. Cami sensed his expectation of this. And then, Connor looked like he would take delight in launching ten levels of hell her way. It would only make things worse. And in any case, why not be honest when the chips were down?

So, Cami shrugged, deciding to play with open cards. "Yes. Yes, I did that."

She saw Connor blink instinctively and felt a brief moment of satisfaction that she hadn't played his game. And a game was all this was. Why was she here anyway? The home page had been temporarily down soon after and then back to normal within hours. She'd checked.

She saw the other agent pushing buttons on his phone, as if sending an urgent message out to someone.

"Were you working with anyone? Were you cooperating with anybody to get this done?" Connor quizzed her.

"I did it all on my own," she replied. She saw his eyebrows raise at that response.

"Why? Do you realize you compromised state security?"

Cami shrugged. "I did it because I wanted to send the message that you don't help people in need." And then, because she was pissed by Connor's aggression, she added, "You guys need to have better firewalls in place. You should be pleased that I tested them for you."

Connor hissed in a breath and Cami saw that had gotten to him. Really, really gotten to him. He'd just had a catastrophic sense of humor failure. Not that Cami thought his sense of humor was his strong point at the best of times.

"You do not realize how serious this is!" Connor said, and now his voice was icy cold. "This is a matter of state security! Breaching this could have caused a major incident. And our security is top notch. You should be asking yourself why you, a US citizen, tried to subvert the security of an official law enforcement site. Security that is in place for a reason! You clearly have no respect for it, do you? You're just a—just a little punk!" At the end, he sounded seriously angry, as if his own control was fracturing.

"Well, okay, then." Cami shot back. This man didn't like her. Didn't like her at all.

And inwardly, she was kicking herself, because she had just worked out what step she'd missed in the hacking. There hadn't been time for a full deletion of her tracks. There had been the tiniest window when getting onto that homepage had been possible. Proud that she'd managed it, feeling mischievous, defiant, and strangely powerful, she'd grasped that window, but she'd left a gap for them to follow her out.

"You know what the prison sentence for this is?" Connor asked, his tone more reasonable now, as if he'd gotten himself back on track.

"Well, of course I know there is one, theoretically," she said.

"Up to twenty years," Connor plowed forward. "Quite often, they'll give the maximum sentence. It's an offense that's taken very seriously. Juries don't like it when people undermine state security."

"What's the point of telling me that?" Cami said, honestly puzzled. These agents surely weren't going to take this further, but they were being far more hardcore than she'd expected.

"Because that's what the law is about. The law is about preventing breaches of state security by hostile forces. If you do that, you're a criminal. A criminal. You have committed a first-degree computer crime, and you have committed a terrorist act against a public safety agency," Connor explained. Now that his anger was under control and his voice was reasonable, the words actually sounded less like a threat and more like a promise.

"You have caused reputational damage and significant financial damage to the FBI as a result of your actions. And that incurs criminal charges. Jail time of up to twenty years for a B felony. And a criminal record that will stay with you for life, following your jail time." He shook his head, as if in disbelief that anyone could have acted so rashly.

Cami listened carefully to his tone, still not convinced by him. Did he really think he was upholding the law? Or was this guy overstepping his mark and trying to get her to go down because of a personal issue he had? Like moves in a game of chess, she tried to think ahead.

She was not going to let him exact his petty revenge. She could demand to speak to his boss. Show him up for what he was doing, especially since time was supposedly so precious to them and this was wasting it. Or she could ask for a lawyer, get the media involved, and start asking why they couldn't take criticism when it came to their unsolved cases. Clearly, the truth hurt them. If she could take this further, it could lead to a big expose.

"You simply do not understand the extent of the seriousness of your crimes," Connor concluded sternly.

"But at least we have a confession," the other agent chipped in.

"Yes. At least we do."

"So, you going to go ahead then?" the other agent said.

"Yes. Let's get going." Connor cleared his throat and stood up. For the first time, Cami was aware that a small tape recorder on the edge of the table was recording this entire conversation, and it had been from the start.

"Cami Lark, you are under arrest."

Cami gritted her teeth. The words shook her, but she wasn't going to show it. She knew this would cause trouble with MIT. They'd be furious. It might delay her graduation. This guy was deliberately meddling in her life, pushing his point, going way overboard.

Well, she wasn't going to let them see that they were getting to her. She was going to stay icy cold, even if they took her down to a cell. Forcing herself to stay as expressionless as if she was bluffing with a losing poker hand, Cami stared him down.

Connor plowed inexorably on.

"You are under arrest for computer hacking and terrorist activity, including breaching state security and malicious activity on a state security site. You have the right to remain silent. You have the right—"

At that moment, the interview room door banged open. They all turned around.

Connor stopped in the middle of reading Cami her rights. A tall, fit-looking man with graying hair walked in, carrying a folder.

"Connor, Thomas," he greeted the agents.

"Fraser," Connor replied, in a respectful way that clued Cami in that this was his boss.

"This is the hacker you just messaged me about?" He glanced at the other agent, who nodded. Then he looked at Cami incredulously. "A college kid? This is her?"

Connor stood straight. "We've got a confession, and we've just made an arrest. I'm reading her rights."

"I need you to wait a moment," he said. Although the words were respectful, the tone was not to be argued with. Connor blinked, looking surprised, and Cami felt a surge of hope, because it looked as if her instincts were right. Connor had been overstepping the mark and was going to get into trouble for it.

But then, Fraser turned to her and stared at her directly with a piercing gaze. Seeing no shred of sympathy in his expression, Cami suddenly wasn't so sure. It seemed like she was still in trouble. Or maybe it was worse now.

"You're still under arrest. But before we take the next step, there's a test I want you to do. Come with me," he snapped.

CHAPTER THREE

A test? Cami followed behind Fraser as he led the way out of the interrogation room, with Connor stomping along at the back.

This situation was twisting and turning like a rollercoaster ride, and she had no idea what to make of it. What was this test about? Should she ask for a lawyer now?

There wasn't time to think about this further because Fraser was turning through another doorway.

Cami found herself in an office. This was a world away from the interrogation room. It looked like a more normal place, but definitely one occupied by a senior employee. It was large, and there was a view of the city through the big window. There was a cluttered desk with a big director's chair on one side, and two smaller seats on the other, and a long filing cabinet with all its doors closed.

On the desk, Cami noticed a photo of a smiling, blond woman and two kids who looked around ten years old. There was another photo of Fraser himself, smiling, with a cute, scruffy black dog on a leash.

So, this guy had a human side, Cami guessed. Could someone who had a cute dog like that be all bad? But then again, he could be a completely different person when he was at work, and she didn't trust people like that.

Before she could get a better look at the photos, they headed to a boardroom table that had six chairs around it on the opposite side of the room.

"Sit," Fraser said.

Cami took the chair he'd indicated and sat down. This seat didn't have a city view. It looked onto a wall with a few framed certificates. Enough to prove to her that this Fraser was a high-powered guy who had a lot of different academic qualifications behind his name.

Fraser walked over to the filing cabinet, and Connor, still looking mad at her, took the seat beside hers.

"I want you to look at this."

Connor looked startled as Fraser walked back from the cabinet and threw down a manila folder on the table in front of Cami, before sitting opposite her.

She looked down at it, then stared up at him. It seemed like he was daring her to say more, and that if she did, he'd chew her out for it. Cami sensed the best thing to do now would just be to shut up and figure it out for herself.

So, instead of asking anything more, Cami picked up the file and took a look inside.

All she found inside were a few printed pages, but as she read through, she saw that this was what she guessed must be part of a murder case.

Feeling a sense of disbelief that this was actually real, Cami took in the facts.

There were two women who'd been found dead, one in a fancy house and one in a top-end apartment. Both had VR goggles lying nearby and a sophisticated gaming setup in their studies, or offices, or wherever they had been found. There were some details on the IP addresses they'd connected from. Not much else though, and Cami wondered if that was because they couldn't get much else. There were small images on printed pages left at each scene. Those were interesting. They looked vaguely familiar to her. Both were the same visual type: attractive female avatars in bold, eye-catching colors. She wondered if the victims were similar too.

It chilled her that this was happening, in Boston, perhaps here and now. But why was he showing her this? What was this test about? Cami looked up at him questioningly.

"You have any further information on this?" Fraser asked.

"I don't know these people. But I guess that's not what you're asking?"

"No, it's not. I want to know—what can you tell me about them? Given what's here, what can you provide in terms of IT information? We think they were both online, and perhaps gaming, at the time when they were killed."

"I can probably tell you something," Cami said. She guessed if they were gaming, they wouldn't have heard a killer break in. That was how he'd been able to sneak up on them, perhaps. And if he knew who they were in the game, and that their characters were online, he would have known when he could get to them. It seemed to her this must be how it had happened.

"In what time frame can you tell me?" Fraser asked.

She shrugged. "That depends," she said. She didn't want to come across as cheeky right now, but geez, they had to understand that she also wasn't psychic.

"On what? On what does it depend?"

"On how soon I have access to a device. I do need a device," Cami explained patiently, watching Connor scowl.

Fraser's lips tightened.

"Get her the phone, please," he said to Connor.

"Her phone?" Connor sounded incredulous.

"Yes. She needs access to a device."

"I don't want to give her back her device," Connor argued, sounding next-level mad. "There's no telling what she'll do with it."

Fraser clasped his hands, looking at Connor with an expression that suggested he was drawing on reserves of patience, but they were not unlimited.

"I'm not allowing her to access an FBI device at this time," he explained. "So, her own device is the only other choice. As she pointed out, she does need to use something."

With an exasperated sigh, Connor got up and marched out of the office. He was clearly heading back to the interview room where he'd left her belongings that had been seized, and Cami felt a brief flare of hope that she might, at last, be reunited with her phone, even if just for a while. Being without it felt as if she had one hand tied behind her back.

She didn't know what this was about. It all felt weird. She needed to find out. If ever there was a time that she needed to be a jump ahead of them, it was now.

Fraser wasn't saying a word and his face gave nothing away.

She felt as if she was in uncharted waters. Actually, no. She revised that. She knew she was in uncharted waters, but someone had thrown her what appeared to be a lifeline. But the lifeline might actually be a disguised snake.

For a moment, she wondered if it might be better to spend a few minutes going through the motions and then say she'd found nothing.

But then she rethought. She couldn't do that. She didn't think she was capable of lying that way. And besides, this was a murder case.

This wasn't just changing the FBI website because she was pissed at them, and she could. This was a serious crime, and it seemed from one of the dates she'd noticed, that it was very recent too.

She had to help if she possibly could. If that was what they needed from her, she'd make the effort, even if she didn't know exactly what the challenge was. Even if they threw her in jail for it afterward, like she was sure they were planning on doing.

She could feel the tingle of excitement in her belly that she got in class when she was up against a challenge that she needed to solve quicker than the others. She couldn't help feeling that way.

It felt like Connor was gone for a long time, but in reality, it was probably only two minutes. And then he was back and sitting down beside her, shoving her phone angrily at her.

With a sigh of relief, she unlocked it and went hunting.

The information in the file wasn't enough, but it gave her the starting point she needed. Her fingers flew over the keys. On a phone, she was a bit slower.

"I'm faster on a keyboard," she explained, in case they were wondering about the delay.

There was an expectant silence in the room, broken only by Connor tapping on the desk. Cami barely noticed it.

She looked up at Fraser.

"How long do you think you'll need?" he asked.

Cami shrugged. "How much detail do you want?" she said.

"Well, let's stick to the basics. How soon can you get information on what they were doing? Their online activities prior to the…to the incidents. The game or virtual reality activity they were in? Is there any way of ascertaining that?"

"The game they were both playing before their devices were shut down is called Bordercross. It's a very popular action and espionage game with distinctive avatars that players can personalize," Cami explained. "This first IP address here uses the name FemmeFatale, and this second one uses VixenThree. Those are their in-game names," she explained. "And those small pictures that were found at each murder scene are their avatars. That's what their characters looked like in the game. What else do you want to know?"

There was a different kind of silence in the room now. A shocked kind of silence.

Fraser looked stunned and incredulous. Connor looked disbelieving, but at the same time, angry, as if he knew he'd only end up making a fool of himself if he did question this.

"You got all that in that time from your phonc?" Frascr said carefully.

“Yes. There’s other stuff I can get, but it’ll take longer. I don’t want to waste your time,” Cami said.

Fraser blinked. She had the strange feeling that for just one moment, he was trying to suppress a smile, like she’d said something wildly funny.

Then he opened his mouth and said something she’d never, ever expected at all.

“I’m going to offer you a deal. We need specific technical expertise on this case, and we need it urgently. It seems you can provide it. So, here’s the choice. Help us solve it and we’ll scrub your record. Refuse, and you’ll spend the next twenty years in jail.”

CHAPTER FOUR

"What?" Cami said to Fraser, incredulously.

She was aware that the same word had burst out of Connor's mouth at exactly the same moment. For the first time ever, and probably the only time, their thoughts had been as one.

Now, Cami saw that Connor was staring at Fraser with exactly the same shell-shocked expression she was sure was on her face. Was this guy for real? He couldn't mean this!

But he returned her astounded gaze calmly. He didn't blink. He didn't look away. He didn't look like he was trying to hide anything. She could tell that he wasn't joking or playing games. Even so, this was beyond what she'd ever thought. She couldn't get her head around it. For a start, how did they expect her to say yes? To this? For the FBI?

Cami felt like she'd had the wind knocked out of her.

Connor was the first one to speak again, sounding incredulous.

"You can't be serious."

Fraser almost smiled. "I'm very serious. She has the skills we need. As of yesterday, our team lost three bright, tech-savvy agents. These are skills we urgently require now in this case. And even though we got some results before Symmons left, he took longer to get the information. She did it in what? Five minutes? Speed will help us now. It'll give us the edge we need."

"But she's a hacker," Connor said in disbelief.

"She's a student," Fraser corrected him. "A student who is about to graduate. Yes, she's hacked in the past. But it's not her full-time occupation." He turned to Cami. "What you do, going forward, is your choice. You're good. You could be useful to us. You could help us on an important case," he said smoothly.

Cami opened her mouth, then closed it again. She waited for a moment, trying to decide what to say.

"Look, I don't want to work for you," she said. "I…I have ethical problems with the FBI."

"You? Ethical problems? With us?" Connor sounded genuinely appalled.

She ignored him as she continued, "I didn't just hack your homepage to cause trouble. I did it because I have an actual issue with you. A grievance. With you as an organization. I don't have faith in you. Or the police, and you're like an even more bureaucratic version of the police. You don't get results. You don't care about the people you're supposed to help. I changed the homepage as a protest. So, I can't take the job. I hope I've helped some in your research, and you find out who killed those women," she concluded, wanting to show sympathy for the victims even though she had no love for the FBI.

She knew this would mean a jail sentence. It was probably a reckless decision, but she had to stand up for what she believed.

"Well, there you go," Connor said, sounding vindicated and also, Cami thought, relieved. "She doesn't want to help. She's just a hacker. Not someone we could ever use, anyway."

He looked at his boss as if thinking Fraser might have been briefly delusional to suggest it.

She anticipated Fraser might look disappointed. That having said some pretty nice things about her skills, he might realize that she had a serious grudge against the organization. That it might give him a picture of how she perceived things.

But no, it clearly wasn't going to work that way. Fraser didn't look disappointed at all but strangely calm.

"You have a grudge against law enforcement. I see that."

"I'm glad you do." Cami nodded.

"I am not going to go into the details about why. I'm guessing there's a valid reason for it—in your perception, anyway— and that you do have a genuine grievance. Perhaps you didn't get closure on a case that someone close to you was involved in. That happens."

She felt surprised. Fraser was being more perceptive than she'd thought.

"Every organization is made up of people. It rises or falls on the shoulders of the people involved in it. We can't solve every case. We do try our best. Unsolved cases are something we hate. Right now, there are people sitting in your situation. The friends and family of the women who have died. They're looking to the FBI to solve this, to give them closure. And we are giving you an exceptional chance, a deal that can keep you out of jail, because we currently have a skills shortage. You have the skills, right now, that could help catch this guy. And that can bring some comfort to those grieving people. You see what I'm saying?"

Cami did, in fact, see. His logic was sound. She nodded as he continued.

"You can't criticize the FBI for not being good enough, when you've been given a chance to be part of it, to add value, and to change it for the better. And you've said no. So, from now on, if you do say no, you have to live with the reality that you chose not to help. You chose not to contribute your skills. You've criticized without being willing to help. And you'll be thinking about that from a jail cell." His face looked so stern and hard that she blinked. "There are no further options for you, Ms. Lark. It is jail, or it is this offer. A deal like this happens very rarely."

He glanced at Connor, who nodded his agreement as he continued.

"We've arrested probably a hundred people statewide, in the course of this year so far, for interfering with FBI business, for attempting to sabotage us in various ways. Do you know how many have been offered a second chance?"

Cami shook her head.

"Not one of them. This is not a common occurrence. The FBI seldom strikes deals. Right now, this is an opportunity for a win-win situation. We both benefit. But it's your choice. It can be a lose-lose, but you'll have to live with the consequences."

Cami stared at him, at a loss for words. He'd made her rethink her own principles through his calm logic, pointing out to her that this was in fact her chance to change things. And the reality was that jail would be terrible.

There was no way she would be allowed access to her phone in there. She probably would not be able to complete her studies. Her life as she knew it, as she dreamed and planned it, would be over, and that truth was suddenly scary to her.

As if he sensed her inner turmoil, Fraser continued.

"We'll organize you a stipend to cover your expenses while you work. We're not unreasonable, as long as you don't renege on your side of the deal. When the case is solved, we call it quits. We drop the charges. No record and no jail sentence."

He steepled his fingers and stared at her again.

"If you help solve a serious crime, you might save more gamers from murder. Families will have closure. You'll be able to get your degree and graduate. You'll have your life back." He paused. "Your choice."

Cami was stunned. If she'd known her own actions would end up with her sitting here, being offered a choice that actually wasn't a choice at all, there was no way she would have hacked that homepage. No way.

Fraser was right. It was an offer she couldn't turn down. Jail aside, from now on she'd have no right to criticize the FBI if she'd refused to help.

She didn't want to let them bully her, but she realized she had to accept the offer. And deep down, she was surprised how sorry she felt for those two women. Being killed while gaming, being hunted online and then targeted in real life—that was evil. Whoever had done that was truly evil. Not just useless and incompetent, the way she perceived the FBI, Cami admitted reluctantly.

Even though she didn't think it was fair, and she felt like she'd been trapped and forced into accepting this.

As if he'd read her mind, Fraser continued, reminding her once again of what he'd said earlier, his voice serious. "The only reason I am giving you this chance is that we need IT talent. Our IT specialists are being lured into IT careers by bright, shiny, exciting tech startups that we can't compete with. I'm putting my cards on the table here. This is our situation, and it's giving you a chance to negotiate your way out of a definite prison term by providing us these skills."

She took a deep breath, her mind spinning.

"Okay," she said. "In that case, I accept your offer."

Fraser's nod of approval coincided exactly with Connor's furious snort.

"Great," Fraser said. "You'll be working under Connor's supervision." There was more than a hint of sarcasm in his words, but Cami felt her stomach plummet all over again.

"Me?" Connor said incredulously.

"I want her working with our most experienced agent," Fraser said to Connor. "This case is top priority. You have our highest solve rate, and I need you on it. What you don't have, in terms of tech knowhow, she can provide."

"But her?"

Connor sounded the same way she felt. Working together with this guy who actively hated her? She could see her own consternation reflected in his eyes too. This was such a bad idea. It could only spell disaster.

She opened her mouth to object. To say, "No, I don't want to be partnered with Connor," but she knew it would be futile.

Fraser, smiling benignly now, seemed oblivious to both their trauma, even though Cami was sure he was fully aware.

"Now that you've accepted the deal, I think it's time for you to get to work. I think we can all agree that catching this killer is of paramount importance to the FBI."

Connor, who was giving her an angry, unhappy look, nodded.

"I'm going to get the paperwork in order so that we can sign the agreement. A legally binding agreement," Fraser emphasized to Cami sternly. "And while I'm doing that, here's the full case file." He placed a larger manila folder on the table. "This is all the paperwork we have on it. There's information online too. I need you two to go next door, to the boardroom, and look through everything we have." Now there was a more intense note in Fraser's voice. "From this moment, the case is yours. And the clock is ticking. You have to locate, and hunt down, this serial killer before he kills again."

CHAPTER FIVE

Cami felt a stab of apprehension as she got up and walked out of the office, heading in the direction Fraser had indicated. This was all happening at the speed of light. Within the space of an hour, she'd been an ordinary student going about her day, and then she'd been an arrested felon, and now, she'd accepted a deal that would see her becoming a co-opted FBI assistant and catching a killer.

Catching a killer. It was never something she'd imagined herself doing. But now she looked back, she guessed she'd always wanted to see justice done. That was definitely a strong part of her character and mindset. She just wanted to do it her own way and not as part of this organization.

"On your right," Connor's iron-hard voice sounded from behind her. Cami veered right into the boardroom. Connor followed, holding the file.

Looking at his disapproving face, Cami felt riled all over again. This was what the FBI was. Men, like this, who only knew bureaucracy and who had a grudge against anyone who tried to be or look different.

This was not going to be easy, Cami knew.

Connor threw the folder on the desk.

"Read through it," he snapped. "Get on board with the background of the case. You're going to need to know the facts so well that you can recite them in your sleep."

Cami opened the file, reading about the two women. Now they had faces and names. Liz Hughes. Adriana Knight. One of them, Adriana, lived only a couple of miles from Cami's digs. In fact, she had resided in the row of fancy houses that was on one of Cami's walking routes from downtown to the university. She liked walking that way, liked the tall trees and the openness of the park opposite. But never had she thought that a killer had walked the same route, broken in and committed murder.

As she was reading through, Connor started talking as if he didn't trust Cami to be able to understand the file's contents.

"Both these women were online at the time of their death, and the killer must have known how to locate them. We assume they were both wearing AR goggles at the time, which would have camouflaged the sound of the killer entering. Both the homes were broken into. Since both victims were in their gaming areas at the time they were attacked, he was able to get close without being seen or heard. There's very little signs of a struggle in either scene. Only a few scuff marks. Filaments under the victims' fingernails that indicate he was wearing gloves."

Despite herself, Cami shivered. Thinking of the victims clawing at the killer's hands was spine-chilling.

"Apart from both being gamers, the women have nothing in common that we have been able to ascertain so far. No contacts in common. From the routine questioning we've done of neighbors, friends, and relatives, there's been no trouble or issues in either of their lives that could point to a motive for murder."

Well, that was obvious wasn't it, Cami thought impatiently. It was very clearly an online connection, given the circumstances, and she was surprised they hadn't pursued it more aggressively.

But then she remembered that they hadn't been able to because these recent resignations had left them short staffed in the tech department. The FBI hadn't been able to, but she could.

At that moment, Fraser walked in with a sheaf of documents. Bizarrely, Cami realized the stack of paperwork she was having to sign here was bigger than the bundle of pages in the case file.

Fraser saw her surprise and raised an eyebrow.

"This contract," Fraser said, "is a legally binding agreement that means if you step out of line, you'll be a felon and you won't be able to use your hacking expertise to do anything about it. Only if you complete your side of the deal, will we drop the charges. You'll be legally bound to stay within the FBI's stated directives. If you're not willing to do that, we don't have a deal."

Fraser passed over the documents and a pen.

"Think about it," he said, as if he was giving her a choice. "If you're ready, we can sign right here."

Cami thought he was prepared for her to argue but right then, she was done with arguing. It clearly wasn't going to get her anywhere, so she wasn't going to give him the satisfaction of seeing her try.

"Sign here." Fraser pointed, and Cami obediently signed. "Sign here." Fraser pointed again. "And here."

Cami took the pen and scrawled her name.

She was committing herself, signing herself over to an organization that she had despised for years. Her name in her own handwriting on a contract she never would have chosen to enter into. Partnered with someone who hated her and who she sensed was going to try and make sure she failed.

Her heart sank. Maybe this wasn't going to work out, and she'd find herself in jail soon.

"Thank you," Fraser said. He shuffled the documents together and walked out.

Connor then checked his watch.

"We need to get to the pathologist's offices," he said.

"The pathologist's offices?" Cami repeated, pushing back her hair in confusion.

"To view the bodies. Because going online is not the only way we can track this killer. There could be some clues for us in the bodies. Some trace evidence. Some indication of who he physically is. And that's where we're going to go now."

When he said "we," he didn't mean her, Cami assumed. There was nothing she could do in that regard. Perhaps she could find out more on the gaming side.

But she saw that Connor was waiting expectantly at the door.

"Come on," he said.

"Me?" she asked. "But…but isn't that your area of expertise? I mean, I won't be able to do much."

He shrugged, looking satisfied for the first time that day. And Cami knew that was because he'd seen she felt out of her depth. She felt worried about where they were going. And he was meanly pleased about it.

"You're under my supervision, and right now, I have zero trust in you. So, where I go, you go."

His voice was without any mercy. With misgivings surging inside her, Cami got up. Clutching her phone, she walked to the door.

She was about to view dead bodies for the first time in her life. And worse still, she was supposed to be looking at them and picking up clues of how they'd died?

Cami swallowed, feeling sweat suddenly chill her forehead.

This was really bad. This was the worst job she could ever have imagined. And she had a sinking feeling that Connor was going to do his best to capitalize on her discomfort.

In fact, Cami feared that this trip to the pathologist's office might even be part of his strategy to force her to quit.

Connor didn't want her as his partner. He wanted to see her in jail and thought she deserved to be there. Looking at his face, Cami knew he was going to do whatever he could to get her there, starting now.

CHAPTER SIX

Cami walked to the elevator feeling as if she had leaden weights attached to her feet. This all felt as if it was spiraling out of control. She hadn't signed up for this—or had she? She had a horrible feeling that every single detail of her new job and her responsibilities would all have been listed in the documents she'd just scrawled her signature over so fearlessly.

From now on, she was bound by the rules she resented, because she associated law enforcement protocol with her bullying, policeman father.

Practically the only thing that kept her calm, strangely, was thinking about those women and that killer. Let Connor drag her all around the country looking at dead bodies. He was just doing it out of spite, to try to get her fired and put in jail.

She'd have to go along with it, but in her mind, she was turning over scenarios. Trying to work out who this killer was and why. To work out ways to catch him. Surely, if she tried hard enough, she could find a way.

For now, though, she had to get through this.

The elevator pinged. They were at the ground floor, but instead of heading directly to the exit, Connor veered right.

"Come this way," he snapped.

Cami followed him as he headed down a side corridor that led to a small room, like a utility room. She could see shelves filled with equipment inside. A man who looked about forty years old walked over.

"Connor," he said with a smile. "What do you need?"

Curiously, he glanced at Cami, as if her appearance was unusual and surprising in this environment. Yet again, she felt herself bristle inwardly.

"We need some clothing." He glanced at her. "A jacket. And a hat." His voice was filled with disapproval as he took in her hair.

She was going to have to wear an FBI jacket? And have her hair crushed down under the blue baseball cap he was now handing her?

Cami felt incredulous about this. It felt like all her identity was being smothered.

"Sure. Anything else? Shirts?"

"Not necessary," he snapped, and Cami realized intuitively that it was because he didn't think she'd last more than the next few minutes.

He literally did not think she was going to be here for long enough to need anything more than a jacket and hat for the trip to the pathologist's office. That was the clear message that Cami was getting.

She put the hat on her head and pulled on the new-smelling jacket without a word.

Then they headed for the parking lot, where Connor's car was waiting—or at any rate, his work vehicle. Cami now saw, as she got into in the front seat, that there was a radio inside and a few extra gadgets on the dash. So, she guessed this was an FBI unmarked vehicle that he was using.

"At the pathologist, we will be speaking to the coroner who did the autopsies on the two victims," he said as he drove out. "We'll hopefully get information that will tell us more about the killer, the time of death, and maybe some other details."

Cami bit her lip. The autopsies. She was going to have to see the women's bodies. And the thought immediately made her feel sick. Thoughts of Jenna flared in her mind. Her biggest fear was that her sister had died and that her body had never been traced back to her family. That she'd ended up an anonymous and unidentified corpse in a morgue.

Cami stared out of the window, looking at the cityscape flashing by and feeling more and more lost.

"I don't need to do this," Cami said. "You're just making me because you think it will put me off."

Connor gave a joyless nod. "You deserve to be in jail."

"Well, I'm not," Cami flashed back. "I'm helping you."

"You are not the caliber of person to work on a murder investigation, even as an assistant. I can tell that. I knew that from the time I saw you," he stated baldly. "There's normally a selection process and rigorous training to become an investigator. Still more to be an FBI agent. It weeds out unsuitable people. Like you.

"What?" Cami asked, feeling offended. "Unsuitable?"

"You're too young. Way too immature. You're too anti-establishment."

His critical words cut like knives, and before Cami could get her thoughts together to respond, he plowed on. “Fraser had a good idea in seeking IT talent. He just picked the wrong person. But that’s okay. Before long, you’ll cave under the pressure. You don’t have what it takes. And I’m not going to go easy on you. The opposite. You don’t deserve to be here. The sooner you’re gone, the better. I want to work with somebody who can drive this case forward with me.”

He sounded threatening.

“Good luck finding all that with IT ability thrown in,” she shot back at him, feeling scathed by his words.

Cami knew he intended to make her life as miserable as he could. If camping out in the morgue was what it took to make her quit, he’d probably try and force her do it.

Who was this man, anyway? What right did he have to criticize her personally when he knew nothing about her? He hadn’t even bothered to ask. At least Fraser had intuited that she had a personal history and a reason for thinking the way she did. Connor clearly didn’t care. Well, if he could criticize her personally, she could do the same.

She took out her phone and stared down at it.

Connor. What was his first name? Here he was. Drew Connor. This had to be him.

Doing a quick search, Cami raised her eyebrows.

“Marriage didn’t work out? Divorce finalized two years ago, I see.”

The car swerved sharply. Cami gripped her phone as Connor got it back under control.

“You seeing anyone else? Oh, wait. Yes, you are. As of six months ago. Nice. She’s an interior designer. Brianna Leach. How’s that going? I see you booked into Figaro’s restaurant recently. How was the food? I can probably find out what you ordered if you give me a bit more time.”

“What the hell are you doing?” Connor spat out. “How are you accessing this?”

“Just looking you up,” Cami said innocently. “I have my ways. I thought I’d better get to know you. Build up the relationship, seeing you are so keen to break it down, and you think I’m immature anyway, so if you want to resort to playground tactics, I’m ready to play that game.”

“Get out of my personal information,” Connor seethed.

"I'm only searching the public domain. So far," Cami said. "I wouldn't dream of doing any other searches on my partner. Seeing we're working together and all."

She thought her threat had gotten through to him. At any rate, his jaw was clenched tight enough that she thought it might snap. If she was going to have her life made a misery, then she was going to give as good as she got. She was not a pushover, and she was not going to be bullied by this angry technophobe.

There was a tense silence for the remaining mile of the drive. Cami felt a queasy mixture of triumph and expectation.

She thought she'd won this battle, but she was very sure she hadn't won the war. And in fact, she'd intensified the conflict. Probably that hadn't been a good idea, even though she'd wanted to give as good as she was getting. Now she'd have to wait to see what the fallout would be.

Connor pulled up outside the pathologist's office. Cami stared at the imposing, square building shielded by a steel-barred fence.

She'd seen it before, driven past without really thinking about the fact that it had dead bodies stored inside, and that this was where people with masks and scalpels probed the secrets hidden in the evidence of violent crimes. She'd never really explored that line of thinking.

Connor parked outside, showed his badge to security at the main gate, and walked in with Cami, now feeling slightly lightheaded from stress, hurrying behind.

The building felt oppressive. The smell of disinfectant was pervasive, and it stung her nostrils from the moment she entered. People in white coats and PPE were walking purposefully down corridors. She heard the murmur of voices in the background and the rattle of stretcher wheels.

"FBI," Connor said. "We're here to speak to Dr. Minnett. She handled the autopsies of Liz Hughes and Adriana Knight."

"Dr. Minnett. She's in examination room five," the receptionist said, pointing down the corridor. "She's wrapping up an autopsy, so she should be able to speak to you."

Connor veered to a cupboard at the corner of the room.

"Mask, gloves. Put them on," he said, taking the items out of the cupboard and handing them to her.

Without a word, Cami put on the mask and pulled on the gloves.

She felt glad, in a way, that the mask concealed her face. She breathed in deeply, trying to quell the surge of nausea.

This was like all her deepest fears come to life, because in this place, the harsh truth of her sister's disappearance seemed to be driven home to her in full, stark detail. She could have been lying in a place like this. Might have been. An unidentified body. That fear erupted in Cami's worst, most vivid nightmares.

Suddenly, she knew she couldn't go through with this. Not with the thoughts of Jenna now crowding her mind.

But she had to. She couldn't show weakness in front of Connor, but there might be no choice there. As she followed him into the autopsy room, forcing her wobbly legs to move, Cami knew that there was no way she was going to get through this without blacking out or throwing up.

There was no evidence of any compassion in Connor's face as he marched forward. And why should there be, she realized. He didn't know her background. He didn't know why she was afraid, genuinely scared, of going into that mortuary room.

She hesitated at the door, feeling blindsided by a wave of nausea.

His expression was like stone as he turned to her.

"You have to follow me in," he said. "Where I go, you go. I'm not letting you stay out here on your own. I don't trust you. And whatever is inside there, prison will be worse. A lot worse," he said meaningfully. "This role can end, for you, at any moment. Fraser might have taken you on against my will. But he will listen to me if I tell him that you are not cutting it. If you need to be fired."

He indicated the door. "You first."

CHAPTER SEVEN

There wasn't the slightest room for negotiation. Cami knew that her entire future rested on a knife edge. Feeling sick, trying to block out the memories and shadows of the past, she opened the door. It led into a short, brightly lit, squeaky clean corridor that smelled strongly of disinfectant. Ahead, a door opened, and Cami saw a masked, gowned, and gloved woman whose face she could barely see, but who looked fair-skinned and petite. This must be Dr. Minnett.

"Connor. Good to see you," the woman was saying enthusiastically. Come through." She gave a polite nod at Cami.

Connor didn't introduce her by name.

"This is a temporary worker, co-opted for the case," he said.

Minnett opened the door, and a wave of cold air washed over Cami, letting out the sickly smell of disinfectant with another odor that she could clearly pick up and which made her gut twist.

"I have the report here." Dr. Minnett pulled a file out of a steel drawer near the room and started to run through the details.

Breathing deeply, Cami tried to quell her nausea, even though the room felt as if it was spinning. She had to do this. She had to be strong in here, even though it felt like the worst experience of her life. She leaned against the wall, sucking air in through her mask, hoping that the room would slow down before the walls tilted too far over.

The atmosphere was what she expected: frigid, clinical, and unwelcoming. Her eyes shifted away from the two steel examination tables. Shrouded forms were on both. But she was sure, at least, the covers wouldn't be pulled back. Not if the examinations had been done.

"The first victim, Liz Hughes, is thirty years of age. Height, five-foot-five. Weight, one hundred and twenty-five pounds. Cause of death, asphyxiation. No signs of struggle or bruising."

"And the other details?"

Through her panic, as Minnett spoke again, Cami could ascertain that now Connor sounded intrigued, engaged, and fully on board. It was as if he was in his element here. As if he could not wait to hear more.

As if all this input, in this chemical-smelling room, was for him the building blocks that would solve this case.

"The killer is a man of average strength. From the marks on both victims' throats, it's clear he's right-handed. Look here."

To Cami's horror, Dr. Minnett now detoured briskly over to the examination table. She drew the sheet back, and Cami flinched. For a moment, she thought she really would black out. She dug her fingers into her palm, and the painful bite of the nails helped ground her.

"You see here on the body of Adriana Knight in particular. There's evidence of pressure on the right side of her windpipe, and from the thumb marks, we can ascertain she was attacked from the front. But because she would have had a headset on, she wouldn't have known 'till it happened."

Cami stared, horrified. On the slab was a woman who didn't look a lot older than herself. Although Cami could see she was a different league. A different life.

She felt chilled by the look of her, by that blank stare. And yet, there were features that reassured her, that grounded her in her panic.

The number of piercings in her ears. The short, edgy hairstyle and the splash of deep blue among the cool bronze hair color. This woman had liked her accessories, even though the earrings had been removed. The tattoos on her forearms were pretty. She had an owl and an eagle, expertly done. She hadn't been scared of what society would think. She'd done what she wanted, and in a weird way, Cami wondered if she might have been a friend. She felt a connection with this victim and suddenly, these killings felt more personal.

"Any prints, any trace?" Connor was saying, his voice urgent and intense, as if this really mattered.

"Nothing yet," Minnett said sadly.

Suddenly, Cami was like a zombie, holding back tears and fighting the urge to bolt. The memory of her sister surged again. Desperate for a distraction, she walked over to the tray that was placed on a table to the side of Adriana's body.

There was the evidence, neatly stacked in the metal tray. The clothing she'd worn. All her jewelry carefully itemized. She'd liked silver, too, Cami saw.

And a phone. That was interesting.

"Thanks," Connor said. "You've been a big help."

"Always happy to help the FBI," Dr. Minnett said, looking at Cami with a slightly curious smile. "You taking a look at the other evidence? New agents are always so eager to get involved."

Already, as she reached for the phone, she could sense Connor's disapproval, hitting her like a tidal wave.

"She's not an agent," he snapped.

"Can I have a look?" Cami asked. Finally, she was on familiar ground. Finally, there was something she could actually focus on, something she could do, without needing PPE or a degree in anatomy or years of experience in staring at corpses. The phone felt like a friend. Her area of expertise.

"Sure, you can. But it's locked. There's a passcode needed." Minnett sounded regretful. "It was on her person at the time of death, in an inside jacket pocket and hidden under her when she fell. It was turned off at the time we found her. There was no phone at the other murder scene, so we assume the killer took it, but didn't find this one."

"Cami, don't interfere," Connor said, sounding exasperated. "It's a waste of time."

She didn't want to be some kind of slave to his commands. She didn't want to be someone who just did what she was told. Not when, possibly, she could do what she knew was right.

There was a technique she could use. It was quick, brutal, and it often worked on phones like this, in her experience anyway. If you flooded the password field by typing in a massively long series of numbers, you could force it to fail, and temporarily override it. She'd done it once before. She'd also failed once. Let's see if third time was the charm, or not, she thought.

Quickly, Cami gave it a go.

She could feel Connor's eyes on her, as if there were a spotlight on her, as if her hands were burning hot.

"It's always frustrating to have evidence we can't access, especially in this case, where time is so important and there's probably so much critical information right there," Minnett was saying to Connor in a conversational way. "We'll send it through to forensics just now and they'll be able to—"

"I've done it!" Cami said with a rush of relief. If there was ever a time when this hack needed to work out, it was now. And it had.

"You've done what?" Minnett asked, sounded confused. Connor was glaring at her, but he also looked uncertain.

“I’ve opened it.” Cami swiveled the phone around to show them, feeling a moment of satisfaction at their astounded faces.

There was the screen, brightly lit, with a modern art painting as the wallpaper. Finally, she felt a surge of confidence after this tortuous experience of being in the autopsy room, and she continued, “So, where do you want me to look first? What do you want to know?”

CHAPTER EIGHT

Special Agent Connor couldn't comprehend that this student, this hacker, had been able to access the phone so fast. Had it really been locked? he wondered. How on earth had she managed to do such a thing?

It was standard protocol that phones were sent to the techs, who would then run programs, and hours or days later, would usually be successful in opening them. For the last few years of his career, that was how this step had worked.

Now she had turned that upside down in just a few seconds.

He glanced at Minnett, seeing her own shock reflected in his eyes.

Now that the phone was open, it could provide valuable information. That was especially the case since the other victim's phone hadn't been found.

The young MIT student was staring down at the phone, looking strangely happy, as if she'd been briefly able to forget about her surroundings: the sharp-sour disinfectant smell, the shrouded bodies with one sheet pulled back, the bright lighting, and the chill in the air.

"How did you do that?" Minnett asked curiously. "How did you unlock it so fast?"

Cami sounded proud as she explained. "This particular phone has a programming weakness. It's possible to overload the system, and by doing that, you can bypass the password request if you do it fast. But there are a lot of different ways for every phone. Some models are much more difficult than others. I got lucky here."

What was she saying? Connor frowned as he tried to make sense of the process she'd used. "Let's go outside," he suggested, realizing that the autopsy room was not the place for this discussion.

He saw Cami look extremely relieved as they all stepped outside. She'd been very out of her depth in the autopsy room. To give her credit, he thought briefly and surprisingly, at least she'd tried. She'd given it a go.

It still had an institutional feel in this side office, but he guessed that to her, it was more normal. There were two desks, a few chairs, and a bookshelf.

"I'll leave you to it," Minnett said, rushing back into the autopsy room. Connor turned to Cami.

"You saved us some time here," he added, giving credit where it was due, even if his voice sounded grudging.

"What about the other phone? Was it nowhere?" she asked him.

"It was nowhere to be found. Our techs did try to track the number. It was turned off. So, in that case, the only thing we could do, which we've done, was to request all the information on the messages, texts and so on. That we've done, but there's an inevitable delay."

Cami raised her eyebrows. Connor could see she was coming to the same conclusion as the team: if this killer had taken a phone, it could mean there was information on the phone he didn't want them to know.

"Right, first things first. This phone. I want to check out the numbers that have called in, the texts, the photos," Connor said, his hand on the phone as if he were already reading from it.

"Well, go ahead." She handed him the phone.

He took it, feeling amped. This had given them a massive head start. Now to find out if any of the messages, any texts, anything he could see, were suspicious.

"I'm going to do a run through the numbers and the texts first," Connor told her. "I'm looking for anything out of the ordinary, anything threatening.

Now that he was in the phone, Connor knew he was on familiar territory, and was confident of where he needed to hunt. He was also aware that there was a ticking clock on how long he had to get it done.

He was very aware that hacking into the phone had given Cami the reprieve that she'd needed. She hadn't been useful in the mortuary room at all, he had been thinking while she was there. She'd hung back, looking nauseated and completely out of her depth. She'd been too afraid to contribute. He'd dealt with young agents and interns before, and it was all about attitude and willingness to overcome their nerves and cope with the realities of the job. None of them had behaved the way she'd done.

Before they had left the room, Connor had been ready to make the call to Fraser, saying that he wasn't prepared to work with her anymore, that she didn't have what it took and never would.

But then she'd opened the victim's phone. And that was something he would never have thought possible. It was a critical move. If it wasn't for her, they wouldn't have gotten the information so fast.

So, he guessed they were going to be working together for a while more, because after showing how capable she was in that regard, and using her initiative in trying, he couldn't exactly complain.

Now, with his focus on the texts, Connor went hunting in the terrain he was familiar with.

Scrolling through the texts, he saw most of them were routine. From friends, family, and saved numbers. You got a sense of what to look for. What about this one?

Now this was suspicious, Connor saw, his attention focusing on the message string. He frowned. It was one-sided. And it was certainly a threat.

"What is it?" Cami asked, as he raised the phone to show her.

He didn't reply. Instead, he turned it back toward him, and started reading the text aloud.

"Hey beautiful. Do you look as cute in real life?"

He saw Cami's eyes widen at that. He read the next one.

"Can we meet? I'd like to meet you! Like to organize a meet-up, babe?"

"Oh." Cami leaned closer to look at the text. "That's creepy. How did he get her information? That should not have been available in the game. Do you think he was a player?"

Connor shrugged. "At this stage we can't tell." He read the next one.

"Hey babe. I want to see you as you really are. I'm sure you're hot. How about sending me a pic? Just one? Or must I go looking for myself? You know I can find out what you look like?"

But then, the texts got threatening.

"Why aren't you responding? Am I not good enough for you? You need to learn a lesson. You need to learn some manners when someone finds you cute!"

And a final one: *"Don't think I can't find you. I know how and I can."*

And then there was no more interaction. It seemed like Adriana had blocked the unwanted messager.

But had she done it too late?

"Those texts are really threatening," Cami said to him, sounding shocked.

"They are," he replied with a nod.

"He could have found where she lived," Cami said. "From the sound of those texts, they met online. Do you think he picked up who she was from VR and stalked her in real life?"

"That definitely seemed the intention from that last text," Connor agreed.

"So, who is this guy? You want me to find out?"

Connor held up a hand. "No. Don't overstep our mandate. The FBI databases can provide us with his ID."

He got out his laptop. He saw Cami give the machine, which was a couple of years old, a dubious glance.

"It works just fine," he told her, defensive now. He was due for an upgrade next year. It wasn't like he was working with obsolete equipment, for heaven's sake. Her expression would probably be the same if he'd pulled out an abacus. That was the impression he was getting.

Quickly—all the more so because she was now staring—he logged into the database he needed and entered the cellphone, hoping that the systems would be fast.

To his relief, they were.

"The phone belongs to Guy Vernon. Here's his address. He lives at 34 Beacon Road."

"Just a sec." Now, Connor saw, Cami was busy on her own phone again. The speed with which she worked still took him aback. It didn't seem humanly possible to be able to work at that pace, to type at that rate from a phone? And she'd said she was faster on a keyboard?

In a moment, Cami looked up, and her face was triumphant.

"I've gotten his IP address. And I've cross-checked it. He was a player in Bordercross. His in-game name is Skullhead. He was there! He might have seen Adriana in there, and that was the point of contact that led to him messaging her, in which case he might also have tracked down Liz Hughes too."

Connor felt a surge of excitement. Between the FBI database and Cami's research, it seemed that Guy Vernon—aka Skullhead—was a strong suspect who had a definite link to one victim and a possible link to the other.

"It's time to go and speak to Guy," he said, standing up. "Let's see if this suspect is home."

CHAPTER NINE

Cami was on the way to interview a murder suspect, someone who might actually have strangled two women. His avatar was a skull, and his in-game persona was tall, dark, and handsome. She felt as if she was on the edge of her seat as she climbed into the car with Connor, and they set off in the direction of Beacon Road to where Guy Vernon lived.

Looking at the darkening streets, she was surprised to see that it was already early evening. She still couldn't quite take in everything that had happened since her mid-morning appointment at the studio.

She showed it to Connor as they stopped at a light.

"This is what he makes himself out to be?" Connor said, with a note of incredulity.

"That's right."

He shook his head.

For the first time that day, she felt that she and Connor were on slightly more of an amicable footing. As if he wasn't actively resenting every breath she took, which was the way she'd felt on the last car ride going from the FBI headquarters to the pathologist.

He was, however, making her position very clear.

"Let me remind you. You're not dressed for the role, and you're not trained for the role. In this confrontation, you are to keep back and let me take the lead. Interviewing a suspect can get dangerous. You are not equipped to handle a situation that blows up on us."

"Okay, I'll keep back," she said. Then, risking a question, she said, "What if I think of something to ask him? Something technical? Can I ask him that?"

Connor frowned. "If the timing is right, yes."

"What do you mean by that?" she asked.

"I mean, there's a time to interrupt, and a time when it'll work against things. I don't know if you have any instincts or feel for that kind of a situation. Probably not, because you're more technical."

Was he insulting her? His voice was very matter of fact, but the implication was that she had no people skills.

Cami bristled instinctively. Of course she had people skills! He was implying that all she knew how to do was IT, like she couldn't communicate otherwise, like she didn't have a perfectly good mouth and two ears also!

But then, she rethought. Decided to think logically about what he'd said. Maybe, this time, it wasn't just personal criticism but simply the fact that she wasn't experienced in this. At all.

Did she know how to question a murder suspect? She had no idea how that went down. What would happen if he turned violent? It was so far outside of her field of experience that she had no idea what would happen. She didn't know how to shoot a gun and had never even touched one.

So, for now, she guessed, her experience would all be useless. She was going to be nothing more than a tag-along and a possible safety risk, and she needed to be humble about that and see what she could pick up from watching Connor.

She stared through the windshield of the car. This morning, she'd been thinking about class and her final IT project. Now, she was sitting in a car, on the way to interview a possible murderer.

Had she ever watched a cop show where they'd gone to the suspect's house and interviewed them? She was sure she'd never seen that.

"Are you going to do what you usually do?" she asked. "I mean when you interview a murder suspect? How does it work?"

Connor frowned. "There's no typical way to interview murder suspects."

"No, I mean, are you going to try to get the guy to confess? Which way do you usually angle it? How do you know if he's telling the truth? What if he gets upset? What if he runs?"

"We'll deal with that when it happens," Connor said, his voice deep and low.

He spoke as if he was used to doing this sort of thing all the time. In fact, Cami was pretty sure that he was. It was she who wasn't.

"There's the place," he said with an audible edge of tension in his voice.

Beacon Road looked established and expensive, Cami thought. The homes were set back from the road and most looked to have manicured lawns all around. Lights were shining in several of the windows. Including this home, where they were now pulling up.

Was this the residence of the strangler?

As soon as she got out of the car, Cami's analytical mind began working overtime. She'd pulled up this guy's IP address earlier. Now, she was wondering, how smart was his home? Could she log into anything? A home like this was bound to have online features.

"There's a camera above the door," she warned as they walked up to the large, solid front door. "It's a Techart Nova. They transmit live and also record. One of the best cameras on the market."

She was sure, by now, that camera had picked up the bright yellow FBI logo on Connor's jacket. By now, if he was looking, Guy would know that law enforcement was knocking.

"You want me to try hack it?" she asked, wondering if she could obscure or pause the footage for a while.

"Let's do it the easier way," Connor said.

Reaching up high, he grabbed the camera and pushed it aside.

Cami blinked, surprised and taken aback. "The direct approach, right?"

But Connor wasn't in the mood for humor. "Remember what I told you," he said, before stepping up and ringing the doorbell. The pealing sound resounded through the house.

Cami stood a pace behind Connor, wondering what he was thinking and wondering what would play out when the door was opened.

There was a tense silence. Did she hear music being turned off? It sounded like the faint thump of music might have stopped at that moment.

And then, Cami heard footsteps approach, and her heart thumped in time with them.

The door was opened. She had her first view of Guy Vernon, who might be a killer and who had definitely sent harassing messages to Adriana a couple of days before she'd died.

He was a tall, big, solid guy, easily six-two, with a mop of dark hair and heavy shoulders. He was wearing a black dressing gown. His features were florid and heavy, and they looked flushed.

"Hi there. Hi, hi," he said heartily. "Can I help?"

He was sweating, Cami noticed with interest. His face was covered in a sheen of sweat, and a trickle of perspiration oozed down his temple. He was breathing hard. What had he been doing? she wondered.

"I'm Special Agent Connor, from the FBI." Connor said.

Cami felt tense as she saw Guy Vernon's eyes narrow at the sight of the FBI badge.

"The FBI? What have I done?" Guy said with a haunted look. "What's this all about?"

"We just need to ask you some questions. Can we come in?"

"Oh, yeah, sure, sure." But he didn't look as if he thought this was a good idea. He was not allowing them into his space willingly. That she could see.

Guy Vernon stood back and allowed them into his house.

Cami followed Connor into the house. She looked around. The place was spacious, an open plan. The hallway led straight into a modern lounge, and Cami could see a big console set up beyond, in what looked like the dining room. The screen was set up on a wall. There was a collection of controllers and headsets. It looked well-equipped for online gaming.

For sure, this guy spent a lot of time online. A lot of money on his hobby, she could see immediately from the state-of-the-art equipment. The home was modern and well-furnished too.

"What do you want to ask?" he said.

Cami noted that Guy hadn't sat on the sleek leather couches. Nor had he asked them to sit. He was standing, fidgeting, and still sweating. He looked extremely uneasy.

Connor hadn't taken his eyes off of him. Cami guessed he was as suspicious of him as Cami felt. There was something strange going on here.

"We're here in connection with two recent murders," Connor said loudly, his voice authoritative.

But he got no further.

At that moment, there was a muffled, terrified scream from the bedroom.

Cami froze. Her heart was pounding. What was going on here? What was playing out?

Connor stared at Guy. Cami could see this man was on the edge of his nerves. Something explosive was about to happen. She felt as if she couldn't even breathe.

It only took a moment for Connor to act. And he didn't dash for the bedroom, as Cami had expected.

Instead, he lunged for Guy himself.

CHAPTER TEN

Gasping, Cami realized that Connor had grabbed this suspect just in time, because she saw now that he was about to turn, he was about to run, and Connor had somehow intuited this.

Guy was shouting now, yelling and struggling, but Connor had the advantage of surprise.

He shoved him against the couch, avoiding flailing kicks with his legs. Guy was shouting—thick, angry curses filled the room in his deep, aggressive tones. A wooden ornament toppled to the floor from off the coffee table, clattering onto the tiles.

"Get off me! Stop this! I've done nothing!" Guy was roaring. "Leave me alone!"

And then, Guy was handcuffed. His hands were firmly fastened behind his back. Cami couldn't believe that he'd done that single-handedly, during this struggle. She hadn't even realized that was what he was doing, because she hadn't been at the right angle. Now, it was done, and she felt a flare of reluctant admiration for the expertise.

Connor was breathing hard but seemed otherwise calm. His face was furiously intent, and his eyes were narrowed. He hustled Guy toward a door, barely visible around the corner, that Cami saw led to the guest bathroom. She hadn't even noticed it there. Connor must have analyzed his entire environment the moment he walked in. Guy was shouting and protesting, but using sheer brute force, Connor shoved him inside, grabbed the key from the latch, and locked the door on him.

"Now, let's go see what's going on," Connor muttered to Cami.

He whirled around, racing down the corridor toward the sound of the scream.

As Cami followed Connor down the wide, tiled corridor, she could hear the screams more clearly. They were coming from a room at the end of the corridor that she guessed was the master bedroom. There was the white-painted door ahead.

Did he have a victim inside? What was going on? The sound of those terrified voices had hit her right in the solar plexus. She dreaded to think what she would find when they got through the door ahead.

It was like something out of a nightmare, she thought. It was like something in a fantasy online game, even. It shouldn't be real life, but it was. Now, in addition to the screams from ahead, Cami could hear bellows and bashes from the guest restroom where Guy was imprisoned. It sounded as if he was bludgeoning the door with his shoulders. She guessed that with his hands cuffed behind him, it was all he could do.

The master bedroom door was closed, but not locked, to Cami's surprise. Connor wrenched it open.

The bedroom was large, luxurious, and messy with black furnishings and dark art on the walls. There was the bed, with black satin covers that looked rumpled and disturbed.

And, from under the bed, a hand was groping.

Cami felt her heart stop when she saw that hand, the fingers flexing as if in appeal. A woman's hand. Pale skin. Deep red nails.

"Let us out!" The voice came again. "We're trapped under here! We got in and now we can't get out! Please, help!"

Connor ran over to the bed. He picked up a corner of it. It looked heavy and difficult to move. Cami rushed to help him, grabbing the side, hauling it up with all her strength.

Together—mostly by virtue of Connor's efforts—they raised the bed enough for the two women under it to crawl out.

As they did, Cami stared anew. She had not thought this entire situation could get weirder, but a whole new level had been reached.

These women were prostitutes, she realized. They were heavily made up and dressed in ultra-revealing, colorful, anime costumes and harsh, garish makeup.

One wore red lingerie with a bright blue wig, and the other wore a yellow mini dress and a pink wig. Each had bare legs and high heels.

The one in the yellow dress was clearly in distress. She was sobbing and shaking. She looked terrified. The woman in the red lingerie seemed scared, but more controlled.

Cami didn't know where to look as the two women sat on the bed. The one in the blue wig reached for a sheer sweater and pulled it on. It didn't make much difference to the general level of semi-nudity. She ended up staring at the Persian rug on the floorboards.

"We are just friends," the lingerie woman explained. "We are just friends of…of this man."

"Whose name you don't seem very familiar with?" Connor asked cynically.

"Just friends," she repeated.

Connor sighed. "You're not here against your will?"

"No, absolutely not. We got scared when we heard the knocking. We didn't know what had happened, so we got under the bed."

"We thought he'd brought…er…brought in a friend or something we had not agreed to," the other woman said. Then, realizing what she'd said, she began to cry.

Connor gave an eye roll that Cami clearly interpreted as having had quite enough repetition of the word "friend."

"This your first time here?" he asked.

"Yes," the blue wig woman replied.

"You know this man from before?"

"No, we…we don't."

Connor sighed. "I need you to be truthful. I've got a tech expert here who can hack your phones in five minutes flat and tell you your life history over the past year. If you are lying, I'll press charges. If you know him from before, all I need from you is information and you won't be in trouble. I'm not here because of you. But the truth is what I want."

The blue wig lady glanced uneasily at Cami, as if wondering whether she had x-ray eyes.

Cami was impressed by his matter-of-fact approach. It wasn't like he wasn't recognizing other crimes. It was just that, in the circumstances, he was choosing the approach that would give him the most information on this crime. The murder. The most serious crime.

"Honestly, no. We…we were hired through an online agency. They told us the address and what gear we should wear. It's our first time here."

"Then go. We don't need to question you. Just get dressed and go."

"Thank you," the blue wig lady said. Not needing to be told twice, she stood up and grabbed her bag and made for the bathroom, closely followed by her red-wigged friend.

"While they sort themselves out, let's get back to Guy," Connor told Cami.

He strode back through the house to the guest bathroom, from where Cami realized the crashes had now lessened.

Connor yanked open the door. Guy was now seated sullenly on the closed toilet, with a mutinous expression.

"Get up, please, Mr. Vernon." Connor grasped his arm and led him firmly back into the lounge.

"Look, I can explain. They're—" Guy was now looking more cowed, as if the time-out had given him a chance to regret his decisions.

"Just friends. Yes." Connor finished for him. "That's not why we're here. We're here in connection with text messages you sent to a woman shortly before she was murdered."

"What?" Guy stared at Connor, his face draining of color. "I didn't send any texts to anyone! I don't know why you're here. You guys, you must leave. Now! I want my lawyer. You need to wait. I'm not saying a thing without my lawyer. Seeing as how I'm an innocent man and all."

Cami thought that was a pretty strong comeback. Guy was pushing his point in no uncertain way. If she had been Connor, she acknowledged, she wouldn't have known what to do. She wouldn't have had a clue. The threat of the lawyer was hardcore, surely. And looking at this apartment, Cami had no doubt that he could afford a lawyer.

But Connor didn't even seem thrown off his stride.

"Now, let's not start down that path. Denial is pointless. We have the proof. Lawyers can come later, if needed, when you're in police custody."

"And why should I be in police custody?" Guy shot back.

"Because you sent Adriana Knight threatening messages. You propositioned her and then you sent her deliberately threatening texts."

There was a moment of horrified silence.

"Her? VixenThree? She's dead?"

He'd used her in-game name. Cami wondered if that would prove to be a breakthrough.

Connor gave Guy a look so blisteringly cynical it could have burned a hole in the wall.

"Yes. She's dead. Surprise to you?"

"Yes! Yes, it is. I…I didn't even know her. I met her online. I…I might have messaged her. When drunk, I mean. Just because—well—out of a desire to meet up in real life. I know I'm not a good communicator. Maybe I used the wrong approach. But that's not a crime! I didn't even know where she lived!"

"Give me your phone. Unlocked, please."

That was the non-tech way of doing things, Cami noted, but Guy handed it over without any argument. Cami realized that was because he was totally confused. He'd had the rug ripped from under him.

Connor had timed his attack in such a way that he hadn't been able to think of any reason why not to give him what he needed.

Connor looked through, nodding slightly.

"You clearly found out her phone number. You could have found where she lived." Connor sounded dismissive of this argument. "And you've messaged a few women. I see here that you also messaged the other murder victim, looking to meet up and get close."

Cami opened her eyes wide. Surely that was a common thread.

"Look, man, I didn't even know. Who is the other victim? I don't know!" Now, Guy sounded frantic.

"Maybe you do know." In contrast, Connor was implacable.

"I have no idea!"

"Well, then, where were you last night?" Now Connor's voice was intense. It was scything through the silence, cutting through Guy's horrified gasps.

"And on Sunday night. I need a detailed account. I need you to tell me your exact movements. Your exact timeline. If you have proof, you will provide that proof. Now!"

There was a resounding silence.

Cami felt her heart accelerating. She felt as if she'd been the one interrogated. That was what it had felt like. It had been terrifying and intimidating. It was astonishing to watch the interaction. It was like watching a high stakes game, where there was everything to lose or win.

Her hacking the phone might have gotten them a step further, but it was Connor that had pushed it, who had pushed this guy to the point where he was no longer ready to deny.

Would he confess? Or would he provide proof? The silence stretched to a breaking point.

CHAPTER ELEVEN

Guy took a deep breath, and the tension Cami had been feeling, all the way in the core of her being, eased very slightly.

He'd broken. She sensed it. And he was ready to talk. Now, what would he say? Was the crime about to be solved?

Guy cleared his throat, and Cami waited, feeling riveted that this entire scenario was playing out right here, in his home territory. In this very living room, he was now about to spill what Cami was sure would be a confession.

But what Guy stammered out next, shocked her.

"Last night, I…I was at home. But I can prove it. I was gaming. All night."

Now, finally, Cami thought she was ready to say something. She wanted to come across as hardcore. To pressure him as intensely as Connor had done. But she didn't think she would be able to come across that way. She was starting to realize that it had taken years, in fact decades of experience, to engineer the showdown she'd just witnessed.

She didn't have that, but she did have the ability to point out a potential lie when she heard one. This was, after all, her area of expertise. Especially since those threatening texts he'd sent were surely evidence of a murderous mindset.

"There's no guarantee that it was you, personally," she said politely, seeing Connor's gaze immediately swerve her way. She hoped she was doing the right thing. It wasn't that she didn't want to overstep her mark. She still seethed with resentment when she thought about the stupid, bureaucratic rules that underpinned this entire useless organization.

But right here, right now, all she cared about was pointing out this potential loophole, without compromising the tense atmosphere that Connor's questioning had created.

"What do you mean?" he said.

Hoping she would hit the right note, Cami replied, "You could have gotten someone else to play for you. Gaming is done under an avatar."

She glanced anxiously at Connor, hardly moving her head. She just wanted to check his reaction. He was expressionless, though. She couldn't tell if he was angry that she'd spoken or if it was the right thing.

Not the right thing for the FBI, she didn't give a minute of her time for them, but for Adriana. For cool, fun Adriana who could have been a friend. With her beautiful hair and her bird tattoos, the feeling Cami had was that she was a free spirit.

For Adriana, Cami wanted justice. And for Adriana, she hoped she was getting this dynamic right.

At least Guy seemed to be eager to reply to her. She'd touched a chord, clearly.

"I would never have done that!" he said, sounding horrified. "Let someone else game in my name? That's like, like sacrilege!"

"But it's possible. Especially if you needed an alibi. You could have gotten someone else in here. You could even have written a program to fill in for you, if you were really clever," Cami suggested.

"I'm not that clever," he muttered.

"So, I guess it's impossible to prove that this was you gaming last night." Now, in a stern voice, Connor took over.

"Yeah. I guess," he shrugged.

"We need other proof."

Now, Guy was starting to look seriously stressed.

"Look, from last night, I don't know what to say now. You've thrown me. You've thrown me because you've, like, dug holes in my truth!"

"Then give us a better truth," Connor said. "Give us more detail. Did you see anybody last night?"

"Not in the real world."

"And we're not taking the virtual world as being a sufficient alibi. So, let's go back further."

"Further?"

"How about two nights ago? Sunday night?"

That must have been the date of the first murder. Did they have an accurate time frame for it? Cami wondered. Perhaps they did, within a few hours at least. She guessed it would depend on a whole host of things and she had no idea how accurate it was. It might have been in the case file somewhere, but not in what she'd had time to read and take in so far.

"Sunday night?"

"Yes."

"Sunday night I do—I mean, I can—I was with someone. With a colleague."

"A colleague?"

"We maintain casino software."

Cami pricked up her ears. That sounded interesting.

"On Sunday, we had to do a few site visits because not everything can be fixed remotely. The machines, some of them have big issues between the mainframe and the cloud technology. A lot of them are still on-site servers. You have to go in; you can't fix everything via the web. And Sunday night to Monday night is the time we do it as the casinos are the quietest."

"So, where did you go?"

"I'll give you a list. We had a whole stack of issues to sort out: glitches to fi and hardware to upgrade. We started at about ten a.m. on Sunday morning. And we worked through to about midday Monday. It's always a long day when we do that, which is every two weeks."

Cami watched Connor's face. His mind was working in overdrive. She could see him comparing the time frames and assessing what had been said. And she thought, suddenly, that he was coming up against a discrepancy.

Guy's version was colliding with the timing needed to commit this crime.

"You have proof?"

He nodded. "Yes. I do. We were in and out of all the casinos. We had timesheets. There were cameras. I was with my work partner—not the whole time, but we were in the same area. In the server's area. And they don't let us in without security."

Now that he was talking about his job, Cami realized she was seeing a different side of him. Confident. Professional. Not like a man who would hire the two prostitutes that she guessed were still laying low in the bathroom, not wanting to walk out in full view of the FBI. He definitely had two different sides, but now it didn't look like either were murderous.

"Give me the proof. If you give me the proof, and we confirm it, we're out of here." Connor's voice was harsh.

Cami's heart plummeted. This was it. The curveball she'd never expected. An alibi. He'd clearly been able to account for his time in a confirmable way when one of the murders happened.

"Sure. Sure. I'll give you proof."

It was weird, Cami thought. It was like there had been this tower of tension in the air that she could almost see looming, writhing, and practically glowing. And now, it had collapsed. The atmosphere in the room was totally different. It was as if all the intensity had dissipated, bleeding out into the corners and away.

Fumbling through his records, Guy compiled the proof and handed the printed sheets over, forwarding the information that was online and couldn't be printed. Connor received it all with a serious face. He checked it thoroughly, but Cami knew that this would be confirmed. It wasn't the kind of stuff that could be made up on the fly. Connor was just making sure.

And then, they left. Connor had a copy of all the paperwork, presumably so that he could add it to the case file and explain why this suspect had been ruled out.

They walked out into the night. Cami felt the cool spring breeze on her face. She heard the hum of the nighttime traffic. She smelled the rich aroma of food from the restaurant down the road, and the more subtle tinge of jasmine from the plants in the front yard.

She looked around as the front door swung shut, mostly to see if the prostitutes had been let out yet, which they hadn't. They were still hiding away.

But she noticed something, that didn't even register at first, but when it did, it sent a chill all the way down her spine.

She saw the camera above the door.

And she noticed it was facing down again. Pointing at the door.

No way could Guy have redirected it. But someone had.

Cami guessed it must have been done remotely. And it could have been hacked. Someone had been watching.

Someone, who wasn't Guy had glimpsed them arrive and had turned that camera facing down again to watch them leave.

CHAPTER TWELVE

He had other names, other identities. There were many layers to his personality, but the one he preferred, the name he liked the best, was Styx. The river of death.

He was in a game at the moment, making some changes to his avatar and exploring the landscape. It was easy for him—second nature, in fact. His fingers flew as he tweaked and fine-tuned. But as well as being in the game, he was keeping an eye out for things that were happening in the real world.

Styx was a gamer, a deep explorer, and a coder who had some serious skill as a hacker too. He had started off obsessed with creating the most difficult and dangerous games that challenged the intellect of the player. Games that led him down a twisted tunnel of logic.

But Styx soon realized that the games weren't enough. They had never been enough. The chase, the excitement—he had only done it because he could. Because it was an outlet for something darker that lurked within him, something that seemed to be becoming more and more powerful.

The games had not turned him into who he was, that he knew. For a while, they had shielded him, given him an outlet. But it was no longer what he wanted, and he had acknowledged this truth. What ran in him was deeper, and it needed a more physical release.

In the end, he had made the decision to give in. To give in to what he had always known was inside him. He had given in to the darkness and to the twisted fantasies, to the desire to take things away and to take other people's lives.

He started hunting.

He acknowledged the darkness in him. He accepted the urges, and he let them take him.

Because Styx knew exactly what he was. And he reveled in it. He was a killer, but an invisible one. And with his hacking ability, he had skills that would allow him to stay that way.

He imagined himself as the identity he'd built, the deep one, the one he rarely showed as he used other avatars to game and interact.

But the one he preferred was dark—a skull with empty eyes and long, bony fingers. He liked the extremism of it. It was the identity he used when he was hacking.

And Styx had thought ahead, far ahead. When he was hunting, he might get caught and arrested. He might get caught and killed. That was all legitimate risk. But he had managed the risk by thinking ahead, and one of the ways he'd done that was by tracking, and hacking, some of the players that he'd seen were interacting with his chosen targets.

He'd thought to himself that way, he could see if they were being investigated and it would provide him with an early warning alarm.

Now, he switched his screen to the real world. Through a combination of talent and luck, he was watching a sight that he thought was very enlightening.

He was watching a man, who was most definitely an FBI agent, leave the premises of Skullhead, who Styx knew from the gaming world.

Without a doubt, this tall investigator was FBI. The blue, bulky jacket advertised that fact loud and clear, but Styx would have known even without that. He had that kind of a face, that kind of demeanor. The type of man who was a fairly good hunter in the real world, Styx thought disparagingly. Although not possessed of the ability to survive in the virtual world.

But his partner, Styx was less sure of. For a start, frustratingly, he couldn't see her face clearly, because of the angle that she was following him and also because of the large baseball cap, clearly FBI issue, that was pulled low over her head, covering her shoulder length dark hair and obscuring her face. She didn't look like law enforcement. He had no idea who she was.

At night? A baseball cap? FBI didn't wear those at night.

Was she undercover or what? It didn't make sense. She was wearing black jeans and trendy boots, but an FBI jacket? He couldn't place her, and she didn't seem to fit into any pigeonhole in an organization that he knew was all about the pigeonholes.

He'd been monitoring the camera earlier and had experienced a moment of amusement as he saw the two girls, clearly whores, arrive. Skullhead was clearly more of a real-life player than Styx had ever given him credit for.

He'd kept watching, idly amused to see how this would play out and how long the girls would be there for. And also, keeping an eye to see if anyone else arrived.

He thought of Skullhead as one of his canaries, like the canary in the coalmine, an early warning system that he needed to be even more careful.

And sure enough, his canary had done what he needed him to do.

He'd watched both of the FBI agents arrive, and he'd seen them point at the camera, and then he'd seen the tall guy turn it around. And then, Styx had a view of the building's brick wall for quite a while as he battled to get into the camera's controls, which were more complicated to hack than just the viewfinder.

He'd done it, and he had turned the camera, and he'd been rewarded by the view of them leaving. They had clearly not found anything worthwhile in Skullhead's apartment and what was important to Styx, is that by the time they left, they must have known the prostitutes were there. They were FBI after all. Though limited in many ways, he wasn't going to make the mistake of underestimating their intelligence.

They hadn't arrived at Skullhead's apartment because of the girls.

He deduced that because they'd ignored the girls, or at any rate given him a free pass on them, Styx reasoned. Therefore, they were there for something else. Now Skullhead might be a drug user or have other illegal activities on the go, but what was interesting is that the FBI agents were leaving without him.

That logically meant they had simply been there to question him.

And that meant, Styx knew, that he needed to be extra careful. Their IT department must have identified the game where he got his victims from.

He hadn't thought they would be capable.

He liked that game because it attracted a lot of female role players, being more of an intellectual game of skill and craftiness. It was a good hunting ground. He could find another game, but it wouldn't have the same significance or give him the same satisfaction as the one he'd deliberately chosen and was enjoying. He wasn't going to allow them to force him to change his ways.

In the past, he'd always managed to outwit rivals and could see no reason why he wouldn't be able to do so again.

In fact, Styx would have laughed at the idea that he was worried. He wasn't in danger. He was a ghost in the system, a shadow in the virtual world, a master of anonymity. No, he wasn't concerned. He had considered himself practically untouchable.

Anyone who tried to trace him would be wasting their time.

And so, he focused on Bordercross again, moving away from the camera footage that now showed the two girls hurrying nervously out.

He went back into his familiar hunting ground, slipping on the guise of his avatar with the ease and comfort of familiarity.

He enjoyed the game, even though he played it for a very different reason. For him, it was not a game but a hunt.

A hunt that had to be done with the utmost skill and determination, one that required stealth, patience, and ability.

It was an intricate game, one that he knew well, but that was constantly changing. It was a game where he was always learning new strategies and techniques. The way the players interacted with one another was interesting, a complex network of inside jokes, friendships, rivalries, and betrayals. An entire culture of its own that he'd taken the time to understand and fit into.

And he was ready to search for new prey, to go about the adrenaline-filled challenge of identifying a target, and then using his skills to get the information he needed to arrive at her doorstep.

He couldn't wait to play his own game and reach its deadly conclusion, again.

CHAPTER THIRTEEN

"Someone moved that camera remotely, I'm telling you," Cami insisted to Connor as they climbed into his car.

Connor looked at her dubiously. "Surely it could have been the camera monitoring company? Or the security firm? Wouldn't they do that if they saw a camera out of place? Log in and move it back?"

"Would they really?" Cami flashed back at him. "Surely a security firm can't go moving cameras just because they feel like it? The customer must tell them where they want the cameras pointed, right? Wouldn't they check with the customer first?"

Connor shrugged. "We can ask them, but if it wasn't them, and it was someone else, we're none the wiser. But I'll put it on the list. The to-do list."

Cami acknowledged that hacking into a smart device was hard enough. Hacking in and finding who had been there earlier might be possible, but it would potentially take days. It definitely wouldn't be easy to follow a digital footprint that was so many steps removed.

"Is that where we're going now, to work on it?" Cami asked. They didn't seem to be heading in the direction of the FBI offices as they turned down a side road, driving toward downtown.

"No. We're going to check into a hotel that we use when we've got an urgent case on the go."

"Why?"

"It makes it easier. Cuts out the travel time. Using a hotel ensures we can keep working for as long as it takes before getting some rest."

He turned right, and a minute later, drove into the basement parking of a hotel. It was a standard, good, business hotel, Cami saw. One of a chain conveniently located a few minutes away from the FBI offices, and with a restaurant and a few fast-food outlets down the street.

"There's a twenty-four-hour kiosk in the hotel. They sell everything you might need, and if they don't, there's an all-night grocery store down the road. Here's some spending money. You can order room service." He handed her a couple of twenty-dollar bills. "We might have an early start, so be prepared. Do what you need tonight when we turn in, whether it's eat, wash clothes, whatever."

He led the way to the elevator. They rode up and Connor checked in. The place was quietly efficient, with standardized decor and a number of guests who seemed mainly to be business travelers.

Connor handed Cami her key card.

"I'm going to go down to the lounge and review the case files. I don't need you to help. This is my job. For now, get some food and get some rest. I need you functional tomorrow."

Cami stared at him, feeling rebellion flare inside her again.

"Why shouldn't I help? I could call the security company and find out about the camera."

"You need to be an authorized FBI agent to get that information. They won't release it to just anybody. So, you'd need me for that, and I'm too busy. There's too much else to do that can get us further. I might not be an IT specialist, but I can tell you now, that's going to end up being a dead end and a waste of time. And you can't go around hacking into suspects' devices at random, either."

"I can," Cami muttered under her breath. She resented that Connor wasn't taking her, or her idea, seriously.

"Go and get something to eat."

Feeling angry now that she was being blocked at every turn, Cami turned and marched away. She headed to the elevator and rode upstairs to her room, number 823. She noticed that Connor had booked the room right next door. Perhaps that was because he still didn't trust her.

She opened the door and stepped into the sterile, neat, featureless space.

Realizing that she was, in fact, starving, she picked up the phone and ordered herself a burger and Coke. Then she plugged her phone in to charge, and sat down on the bed, deciding to wait for her food before she did anything else.

But almost immediately, there was a tap on the door.

Wondering if this was Connor coming to bother her again, she stood up and headed over to it.

She opened the door, and to her surprise, found herself face-to-face with a fit looking, dark-haired man who looked to be in his mid-twenties. He had an open, honest, and strong face, sort of like an adult Boy Scout, she decided.

He stared at her in surprise. "Sorry. Got the wrong room. I was looking for Connor."

She saw he was holding a kit bag containing some electronics and equipment.

"He's checked in next door, but he's working in the hotel lounge right now," Cami said. Seeing that this man clearly knew Connor's name, and that the two rooms were allocated to FBI, she guessed he must be FBI also, and not hotel management.

"Do you work with him?" she asked.

"Yes. I'm on his team. As of the beginning of this year. You must be Cami Lark?"

"On his team, as of today," Cami agreed, and to her surprise saw a flash of humor in his expression. He had good looking features: hazel eyes and an open intelligence to his face.

"I heard about you."

Cami stared at him suspiciously. So, this guy knew she was a felon who'd escaped arrest? That didn't put things on a good footing. But his next words told her differently.

"You're the IT whiz helping with the case," he said. "That's really cool. Something we need. I know a bit, but not enough. You're at MIT, right?"

"Yes, about to graduate," Cami said, feeling surprised by how the word must have spread.

"Who are you?" she asked, wanting to level the field, seeing he knew so much about her.

"I'm Ethan Myers."

"And you're an agent?" Cami hadn't thought that FBI agents came in this particular package. Ethan was definitely more relatable than Connor. And he seemed friendly too. Normal. He didn't seem disapproving of her, rather more admiring. That was a relief.

"Yes. As of the beginning of the year. So fairly new on his team."

Cami decided she liked him right away. He seemed to be more of a free thinker and less bureaucratic, from the way he spoke so far.

"Why did you join?" Cami asked curiously.

"I began to be motivated by the fact that I could help fight crime. I have, you know, a family background of being affected by crime." Cami sensed there was more to it, but that Ethan didn't want to tell her. At any rate, she felt sympathy for him. She knew what that predicament was like, even if it had sent her the opposite way.

"I was working in IT, but more on the management side, as a project manager. So, I decided to make a move. I wanted to apply what I knew and use it to make a difference," he continued.

“So, you actually applied to join?”

"I applied, and I guess I checked out all right, so I got the job. I went to Quantico for training, and then I joined Connor’s team.”

“And are you working on this case?” Cami decided if he was, it would make life a lot more interesting. But to her disappointment, he shook his head.

“I’m working with my investigation partner on a different case, but we still have to check in with the boss. And Connor asked me to bring along all the equipment. So, I’ll go find him now, and brief him on what we did today.” He hesitated. “Nice meeting you. Nice to be on Connor’s team with you.”

“Likewise,” Cami said.

She watched him walk back to the elevators, feeling more positive. It seemed like there were some cool people in the FBI. Ethan could definitely be a friend. He was cute and smart. And he’d chosen, actually chosen, to join? That surprised Cami.

The elevator pinged again, and this time it was room service with her food.

She ate quickly, remembering what Connor had said about taking the chance to eat, because you never knew what the morning will bring.

Cami had an uneasy feeling about that, based on the blank, implacable eye of that camera.

She remembered how it was tilted down and watching them. Who had guided it there? Surely it must have been the killer. Perhaps he’d been checking up on other people in the game who he knew had interacted with his victims.

If she was this killer, and she knew law enforcement was now tracking down people in the game, she would personally be scared and be looking to cover her tracks.

But she wasn’t the killer.

Cami guessed that if he had seen them, it might inspire him to do the opposite. If he was on a murder spree, and he had seen the FBI arrive, it might encourage him to speed up what he was doing and kill again.

She had a very uneasy feeling that they weren’t going to be lucky enough for a sneaky, psycho guy like this to quit what must surely be an obsession.

She felt worried about what the morning would bring.

CHAPTER FOURTEEN

Cami was awoken by a loud, persistent knocking on her hotel room door. She was so deeply asleep that for a while, her dream shifted to driving on an old country road, with a rattling truck storming past.

Then the phone on the bedside table began ringing and that noise ripped her straight out of her slumber. She grabbed up the phone.

"Hello?" she said blearily. She was not a morning person and—if morning at all—it was still dark.

Connor replied, sounding brisk, energetic, and wide awake. Also, highly stressed.

"Cami, we need to get going. Get dressed immediately. Meet me in the lobby in ten minutes." He paused, and then delivered the bombshell. "There's been another murder."

"What? Another murder?" Groping for the bedside light, Cami knocked over the coffee mug on the table, luckily empty. It toppled on its side with a clatter. "I'll be there now. I mean as soon as I can."

Connor disconnected, leaving Cami to scramble.

She finally found the light switch. Checked the time. It wasn't that early—six a.m.—but it was a grim, gray, and rainy morning.

She climbed out of bed, pulled on the spare shirt she'd bought from the kiosk last night and grabbed her underwear from where it had been drying in the bathroom. She ran her fingers through her hair and pulled on her baseball cap which she had to admit, was a handy fix in this rushed situation.

Another murder? What had happened? When had this person died? Was it exactly the same type of kill? Questions surged in her mind. She knew Connor would be able to provide answers. Some of them, at least.

Barging out of the hotel room with her purse under her arm and her FBI jacket in her hand, Cami sprinted for the elevator and rode down to the lobby. There, Connor was waiting, none too patiently. He was pacing from wall to wall.

"Let's head out," he said.

Still partially awake and totally thrown by the twist that things had taken, Cami rushed after him, down to the basement, where the rainy chill was more intense. She quickly pulled on her jacket as they headed for the car.

"Where are we going?"

"To the murder scene," he said shortly. "The victim is a woman called Kate Warner."

That silenced Cami. To the murder scene? She had feared it, in the back of her mind. This was going to be another experience that shocked her right out of her comfort zone.

Normal life seemed so far away as they sped through the rainy morning. It was still early enough that rush hour hadn't gotten going. The headlights of the light traffic flared in the damp, chilly air.

Thinking of normal life, Cami remembered something with a jolt.

"I'm supposed to have a class at nine today," she told him as they drove out. "A few classes, at MIT. I'll need to call them. What should I tell them?"

For a moment, she imagined waking up in the tiny bedroom in the university's residence hall that until yesterday she'd considered her home. How it would feel to look at her gaming and screen setup on the shelf as she sat up in bed, watching the light filter in through the window. It would feel normal and reassuring. She'd lost that normality without even realizing how comforting it had been.

"You don't need to tell them anything," Connor said. "We spoke to them yesterday."

"You did?" Cami asked, feeling startled. They'd contacted the university already? Something about the speed and high-level efficiency with which that had been done was…well, scary.

"It's all organized. They are aware of the circumstances."

Was Connor deliberately not telling her what, exactly, the FBI had shared with MIT? Did the university know she was a potential criminal? Would it affect her scholarship?

Connor wasn't saying more. Not about that, anyway.

"We have a lot to do right now," he told her. "We're going to the murder scene to see what evidence we can find. This victim was also found in the same set of circumstances. She had a gaming setup; she was found with a VR headset near her body. This is where I'm hoping you'll be able to provide insight that can give us a lead on the killer."

Cami sat straighter. This sounded, at least, as if she'd be able to focus on the IT aspect. If there was anything to find, what would it be? What would she need to look out for?

Suddenly, she realized she was feeling less dread at the thought of arriving at the scene. Instead, there was more of a determination to get some clues that might lead them to this nameless and faceless murderer.

Even so, she couldn't help staring as they drove up to the home. Already, from far down the road in this cozy residential suburb, she could see the flash of red and blue lights through the rain. The police had cordoned off the narrow road, and Connor showed his FBI badge before being waved through. She felt her stomach tighten as they drove up to the house where the murder had occurred.

Four police cars and a few other vehicles were already parked in the road, and a couple of officers were standing in waterproof jackets, managing the scene. The rain was lashing down.

Cami looked around her in growing unease as they parked. Despite the rain, there was a small crowd gathered on the sidewalk. Under the umbrellas and rain jackets, she couldn't see the people's faces. Nor did she want to. This whole scene felt so tense, so fraught. These people had suffered a terrible crime in their neighborhood. There was a sense of shock.

Connor got out, and he and Cami half-ran the short distance to Kate Warner's home. It was a small white house, with a tasteful, old-fashioned front yard—flowering shrubs and bushes, a stone birdbath.

Connor led the way up to the house. They got under cover in the hallway. Immediately, Cami picked up the hum of voices, and from their direction, she guessed that this murder had taken place in the room on the right, down the corridor.

A police officer rushed out, greeting Connor like an old friend.

"Morning, Connor. Glad to have you on the scene," he said.

"Morning," Connor replied.

Getting straight to the point, he then asked, "Who found the body?"

"The cleaner," the police officer said. "A woman called Melissa Perez, who cleans here twice a week. She has a key to the back door. She let herself in this morning, found the body, and called us."

"Have you interviewed her?"

The police officer grimaced. "She was in a state, understandably. We took her statement. She saw nothing. She arrived on the bus. She said the door was open. There's an electronic locking system on the front door, and she wasn't sure how it could have been bypassed, but she said it has malfunctioned before."

Or the killer could have hacked it, Cami instantly thought, guessing from Connor's glance he might suspect the same.

"Thanks. We'll go and have a look at the scene now," he said.

"Before we go through, we need to put on PPE," Connor told her.

He handed her foot covers and gloves. Cami fumbled on the still unfamiliar items, with the plastic feeling weird as she walked. Then they headed down the wooden floorboards toward the murder scene.

Cami took a deep breath as they entered the room, telling herself not to be distracted by the corpse. She must look at the surroundings and focus on her reason for being there.

There were two white-suited technicians on the floor near the body, obscuring it mostly from view. To her relief, she saw that the body lay a couple of yards away from the new-looking computer console on the desk that would be her area of focus, in an office that looked well used. There were files on the table and notebooks in a tray. The victim was lying near an upended chair. Had the killer grabbed her from behind and pulled her backward? she wondered.

She saw dark clothing and a flash of blond hair. She felt a surprising surge of anger that a criminal could have done such a brutal, terrible thing, and in this woman's own home, while she was online and in another world.

"Morning, morning," Connor said.

"Morning, Connor," the closest of the two men replied. "Bad situation with three of these, now. Going to need to contain the panic, and all in Boston too."

"It is bad," Connor said briefly. "Time of death?"

"Probably about ten p.m. last night. No sign of forced entry—there was in the other places. Possible that the electronic lock malfunctioned, or the killer found a way past it."

"Possible," Connor said. "Any evidence, any trace?"

"Nothing so far. We've checked the desk. We did that first, so if you want to work there, go ahead. The computer was turned off when we arrived."

Like the others had been, Cami remembered from the case file.

"Any phone in evidence?" Connor asked, and she thought he was also looking for the parallels.

"We haven't found one."

Connor nodded at the setup.

"Take a look," he said to Cami. "See what you can find, see where she was. Whatever you can get from this setup, might be useful."

This was her time. Her test. Even though she knew Connor didn't trust her and would be watching her closely, she hoped that she could prove her skills now, and shine the spotlight into the darkness where this killer was hiding.

Stepping forward, relieved to be moving into familiar territory, Cami turned on the machines. Blocking out the sights and sounds from behind her, she went on the hunt.

CHAPTER FIFTEEN

This was the first time ever that she'd typed on a computer keyboard wearing gloves, Cami thought as she turned her mind to getting into the system. It was shocking beyond belief that this woman had been murdered, and if there was anything online that could point the way to the killer, she was determined to find it.

With no phone available, any answers to be gained immediately would have to come from the computer setup.

Behind her, she could hear the sounds of the body being moved. There was a whir of wheels as the stretcher was pushed into the room.

She wasn't going to look around, she didn't want to see that, and she felt glad to be able to focus on what was her area of expertise.

She started up the machine, and in the brief few seconds that the fast technology was powering up, Cami made a mental list of what she was going to look for first.

There was a password. That was her first challenge.

Quickly, Cami worked to bypass the system's main access password. It was fairly simple. It didn't take her long at all to get around it. And then, she saw what lay beyond. A setup that looked mostly used for work. In fact, to her surprise, Cami saw there were only a couple of games loaded.

"She was playing Bordercross," she said aloud.

"She was?" The words, from right behind her, made her jump. She hadn't realized Connor was just about breathing down her neck. With a flash of resentment, she wondered if he was there to check up on her and make sure she didn't veer away from her FBI-imposed mandate.

Really? Did he really think at this time she was about to do something else and not look for clues? Is that the opinion he had of her?

But there was no time for Cami to explore the resentment that was now smoldering inside her again. Not when her research was proving to be fascinating and, she hoped, useful.

"Yes. But this is strange. She's a very recent user. Her avatar is called SirenSong, and she created it just a few days ago."

"Now that is interesting," Connor said. "On what day?"

"On Saturday morning," Cami said.

"The day before the first murder," Connor said thoughtfully. "I wonder if that's significant. How about most recently?"

"Yesterday, she logged onto Bordercross at eight p.m. or thereabouts and she was playing from then until the computer was shut down just before midnight."

Cami guessed that would have given the killer four hours from seeing her online to arriving at the home and killing her. Most people gamed for at least four hours, so he would probably have known that he had time. And there was something else interesting, she saw.

"She's recorded all her footage from the game," she said.

"Can we use that? Would she have interacted with the killer?"

Cami shook her head. "Not necessarily. He could have simply noticed her in a public or communal place. That's the whole point of the game, really. It is an espionage game and characters are able to observe situations. But somewhere on the same screen, within sight, the killer would have been visible."

"So, we could track him that way?" Connor sounded eager yet impatient, as if frustrated at his own lack of knowledge.

"It depends on what areas she was in. Some areas, there are a lot of other game players on screen and in view at any one time. Hundreds of others, and you can move from scene to scene. Some scenes are quite crowded if they are public places within the game."

Cami saw Connor was frowning, as he took all this information in. She continued explaining.

"So potentially and most likely, she would have been visible to hundreds of other players so far. But the footage is here if you want it. She's played for about fifteen hours in total."

"Fifteen hours of footage. Hundreds of other players."

Connor sounded thoughtful and she guessed he was feeling the way she was, that this killer was near and yet, so far.

"We can use the footage anyway," he said. "Can you download it, save it somewhere? It'll be time consuming, but it could provide a link to other evidence."

Cami saw the logic there. "Sure. I can do that. I'll create a cloud storage for it and forward everything there."

Quickly, she got that started, feeling relief as she glanced around to see the stretcher getting wheeled out.

"Okay," she said. "I think that's done."

"Good work," Connor said.

"Do you want to look at anything else on here? Now that it's open?" Cami was feeling curious about what Kate Warner did, and why she'd taken the trouble to record every episode of the game.

"Yes. What can you find?"

"I'll have a look."

Cami left the gaming setup and navigated into the other files and folders. It felt weird doing this. Hacking was one thing, motivated by a cause. But this felt in a way like looking into someone's private life. Cami felt a flash of sympathy. Never, twelve hours ago, would this woman have imagined that she would have been killed, and the FBI would be going through her online transactions.

Cami could see several work-related sites here, multiple social media accounts, a couple of storage sites, email, and even a picture folder.

"She's a journalist," Cami said. "That's her job. She works as a senior investigative journalist for a national publication and does freelance work also, from the look of this." Searching through the documents, Cami frowned. "You know, I don't understand why she would have been doing online gaming. Because to me, it looks as if a lot of the articles I'm seeing here are negative toward the whole online world."

"Such as?"

"'Online Poison: The Psychological Dangers of Gaming,' 'Virtual Insanity: the Money behind the Madness,' 'Webcam Worries: The Predators that Lurk.' To mention just a few."

"It doesn't make sense she was playing, then, if she was so anti-gaming. Unless it could be to get background on a story," Connor suggested.

"Yes. That would make sense. If she'd logged in so recently, perhaps she was investigating Bordercross specifically," Cami wondered. That might take them further. Perhaps this game, or its makers, had a dark underbelly, and there was information waiting to be exposed. Journalists didn't go digging for no reason. Maybe Kate Warner had received a tipoff or a lead that something was wrong.

"Can you find any notes? Any current research? What new files are there?" Connor now asked, his voice urgent.

"Let me see."

Cami searched through the documents, looking at the most recent documents and emails.

She felt her excitement rise as she looked at what Kate Warner had been working on.

"Connor, this is weird."

"What is?"

"What I've just found." Joining the dots, she couldn't actually believe what she was seeing. "This might be important. It looks like she was actually doing an expose of Virtual Ventures. That's the gaming company that developed Bordercross." Leaning forward, now riveted by what she was discovering, Cami accessed the working documents and notes. "That might be why she logged into the game and recorded it. To get live background and perspective. But the expose article isn't about the game itself, it's about one of the company directors in particular."

"Which one?" Connor asked, his voice sharp.

"A man called Rowan Andrews. From these notes, it looks like she suspects that Rowan Andrews was stealing the private information of online players and selling it."

There was a shocked silence as Connor took in this information.

"She's gotten quite a lot of proof so far," Cami added, reading further. "It definitely looks like there was something irregular going on."

"Rowan Andrews. Bordercross." Connor repeated. "I'm going to pull up an address for him now. Forward all the information you can get off that machine. All the research. From the timing, this doesn't seem like a coincidence. A journalist investigating the game turns up dead. It could be a targeted murder or even a hit. The other kills could be camouflage, or else the guy had more reason than one for killing."

Cami felt sick. "Do you think Kate was targeted because she tried to expose them?"

"We don't know. But there's a strong link. If Kate Warner was killed because of her interest in this, then Rowan Andrews is a prime suspect, and there's no time to waste in questioning him."

CHAPTER SIXTEEN

Had Rowan Andrews, owner of Bordercross, known that Kate Warner was writing the piece on him? Had he gotten a heads-up from somewhere? Cami guessed that was possible. She decided she'd better find out more about the man they were going to meet. As soon as she and Connor were in the car, she got onto her phone and went looking.

Rowan Andrews, age thirty-four, was a tech millionaire, she learned.

"It says here that he made several million dollars from his online gaming ventures," she said.

Connor raised his eyebrows. "The money that's in tech," he observed cynically.

"He's now a power player, throwing his influence and money behind social causes as well as being a shareholder of several other IT related private and public companies." Cami wondered if that was why he was worried about the expose article.

"What else does it say?"

"It says here that in the past, he has openly admitted to being fascinated by the idea of 'cyber-warfare' and that was a major motivating factor for why he created and financed Virtual Ventures, the company that developed the best-selling game Bordercross."

"So. He's highly intelligent. A self-made man and a successful entrepreneur. Clearly, tech is his playground. But is there more to him? Anything else you can pick up?" Connor wondered aloud.

As Connor joined the main road, rain spattering on the windshield and wipers swishing it away, she went digging deeper.

"I'm finding interesting things here," she said, after a while.

"What are you finding?" Connor asked, glancing over at her.

"That he's ruthless. He has taken over rivals and colleagues that get in his way. He has no qualms about how brutal he can be. He's been part of some very unsavory deals. There's a piece here that was removed from the news website, but it's still searchable in the archives, that mentions he bragged about his mob connections."

"Mob connections?"

"Yes." She saw Connor's frown and looked at him. "He's not afraid to do what he needs to do to get what he wants," she added.

"Sounds like the type who could be behind a hit," Connor said. "Those murders could be hits that he's ordered for different reasons. Or the first two could be a smokescreen for the third. Especially if he's been warned about the investigation."

They were driving out of town now, into a well-tended countryside area that Cami saw contained luxury lodges and exclusive retreats, as well as private mansions, set in large grounds.

Ahead was the home of Rowan Andrews, director of Virtual Ventures.

The gateway was massive, Cami saw. The gate itself was an extravagant, wrought iron contraption, painted silver and black. The paved driveway beyond was made from jet black bricks. On either side, a strip of brilliant white gravel provided a dazzling contrast. Going up the drive, instead of the trees that other properties had, there were massive decals and artworks, depicting scenes and characters from the games.

Their size and garish color gave the entire place an otherworldly feel, and that was before Cami even got around to looking at the mansion on the top of the hill. It was a black and chrome, modern, angled edifice that looked more threatening than imposing.

A private security guard in a black uniform stood at the gate.

Would they get past this barrier? Cami wondered. Connor seemed calm as he buzzed the window down.

"FBI," he said briefly.

The guard looked surprised, and scrutinized Connor's badge carefully, before pressing a button that opened the gate.

They drove up the long drive and Connor parked outside the house.

The entrance beneath the overhang was dark, against a dark metal door, which Cami noted had a camera too. She didn't doubt that already, Rowan knew they were here and was preparing his strategy.

This was a smart home, she saw, noting the keypad by the door.

It would therefore be controlled by a smart hub. Seeing smart homes were relatively new, their security was not as well protected as it should be. One of Cami's projects in her second year had been to innovate ways to make smart home technology more secure and less risky.

Perhaps she could get into the network, she wondered. It might allow her to access his devices if she could. There were two ways of accessing a smart hub. The first was to access the hub directly, and the second was to log in to the home's wi-fi network. Which would work better, she wondered.

She got the searches running, to see if she could find a way in.

Just in time. As she and Connor climbed out of the car, two more guards approached. They wore the same black uniform, with firearms on their belts. They looked businesslike and aggressive.

"Stop there," one of them said. "What are you doing?"

Connor showed his badge, seemingly unperturbed by their threatening demeanor.

"We need to speak with Rowan Andrews," he said. "We want to ask him some questions relating to recent crimes."

"On whose authority?" the guard pressured.

"The FBI's," Connor said easily.

"You know you're on private property? Do you have a warrant?" the guard pressured him.

"We don't, but if you give us a reason to go and get one, it will end up being a far more extensive search," Connor said pleasantly. "At the moment, questioning is all we're here for."

"It's my job to ensure the security of this place. I'm not allowed to let unauthorized visitors in," the guard insisted.

"This isn't a social visit. It's a crime investigation," Connor replied.

"If you enter the premises without permission, you'll be trespassing," the other guard snapped.

Cami could sense these guards were overbearing, bullying types. Was this a delaying tactic to allow Rowan to sneak out of the house? she wondered suddenly. Was that why they had let them in and not stopped them at the top of the driveway where they would have blocked the exit? Were they going to see a sports car speeding up to the gate and getting out in the next minute or two? Cami could picture this scenario easily.

Time was of the essence, and they didn't have time to mess around here.

"We need to talk to him," Connor said.

"I can't let you in," the guard repeated. "Our company and our boss have nothing to do with any crime," the guard said.

"There's a clear link, or we wouldn't be standing here," Connor replied. A gust of rain sent them all edging further under the overhang.

"I'm not going to repeat myself, sir. You can't come in. I'm just doing my job. Come back with a warrant," the guard said.

Cami glanced down at her phone again.

Her hack had worked, but only partway, she saw. The program she'd written had been able to access the main operational password, but not get into the wifi at all. So, his devices weren't accessible. Only the house.

Cami shuffled behind Connor so that she was out of sight of the guards. They weren't looking at her in any case, clearly perceiving the tall, strong Connor to be in charge and the main threat. But she didn't want them watching while she worked.

What would be possible?

Turning the lights on and off wouldn't get her very far. Activating the toaster might be a waste of time if nobody was in the kitchen. Even if it was, it wouldn't do much.

She had a smart home at her disposal, part of it anyway. What could she do? Activate the gate?

Nope, Cami decided. That wouldn't do enough either.

Here was something on the list she could use, though. She had no idea what it would do or if it would have an effect at all. But perhaps it would help. At any rate, it would provide the biggest distraction.

Experimentally, she pressed the button to activate the alarm. A moment later, a sharp, loud siren began wailing out.

Everyone except her jumped at the noise, even Connor. The guards glanced at each other. Cami saw that they looked worried. The kind of worry that a guard might feel, she thought, if the boss was home and a loud, unexpected alarm started sounding.

She was sure that Rowan was inside and that was why they were stalling, but now, the alarm had created a crisis.

"Wait here," the guard said firmly.

The two men rushed away, heading around to the back of the house where Cami guessed the control panel must be.

Connor glanced around.

"Was that you?" he asked incredulously.

"Yes. I managed to get into the smart home's controls. I can't access his devices, though. I tried, but I couldn't get past his firewalls. But I can get to some other things. I can lock the doors, so that they would have to bypass them manually," Cami said. "Once you get into a smart home's control system, you can work with whatever's on the list there. So, I guess the more chaos we can cause, the more chance we have of getting to Rowan."

The alarm stopped abruptly. So, they'd managed to override that because it was no longer available to activate again.

"Give the doors a try," Connor agreed. "Lock the doors. Let's see if we can flush him out to the front."

Cami pressed more buttons. She needed to work quickly, but the rainy weather was delaying the interface. She tried again, as the first command hadn't worked. She hoped the guards were not busy overriding everything manually.

Connor was relying on her, and she did not want to fail him. Right now, failure was surely not an option. She needed to show him that she could do what he now expected her to be able to do. That put the pressure on, especially working at that speed. If she'd had an hour, it would have been different.

There it was, there was the shortcut she needed. With a flash of relief, she activated the interior locking system. It might not do much, but it would slow him down if he was planning to escape by a side door. Especially if the locking control panel happened to be near the front door, which she was sure it was.

"Okay, it looks as if all the interior doors are now locked," she said. "And there's a notification here I can activate. 'Exit Front Door'. I wonder, if I press that, whether it might go through to his phone as a security message? There are several others, but this one will lead him straight to us if he sees it."

"Give it a try?" Connor said.

Feeling expectant, Cami activated the notification. Then she waited.

A minute later, footsteps sounded, and the door was wrenched impatiently open.

"What's going on out there? What's the reason for this message?" a man said irritably.

Cami found herself staring at a tall man with silver-blond hair wearing a red leather jacket, with silver rings on his fingers, and a heavy platinum chain around his neck.

Without a doubt, this was Rowan himself, and she could see the shock in his face as he stared at the FBI agents on his doorstep.

CHAPTER SEVENTEEN

Cami felt astounded that her plan, with Connor's help, had worked. Rowan had been lured to his front door by the message. He hadn't seemed to think he was in any danger, and Cami felt sure that he'd intended to shout at the guards for messing up and activating the alarm.

But now he was face-to-face with them.

His face changed instantly. Looking angry, he made as if to slam the door, but like a flash of lightning, Connor got his foot inside.

"Rowan Andrews? FBI here. We need to speak to you. Urgently," he insisted.

Rowan glared at them both. "I have nothing to say to you," he said firmly.

"You know why we're here?" Connor said.

"No idea. And you're wasting your time if you think there's anything I can tell you," Rowan said. "I'm not going anywhere with you. Now get your foot out of my door. This is private property."

"Mr. Andrews, you need to come with us to provide information we need." Connor stood his ground, but Cami saw, with a flash of worry, that there wasn't going to be much he could do if Rowan kept digging in his heels.

"I'm going nowhere," Rowan insisted.

"Aren't you interested in helping?" Cami said. She saw his focus swivel to her angrily. Hoping to push her point, she stepped forward. "I mean, you're so involved in social causes. The amount of times you've said that you want to help society is all over the internet. And now, you don't want to come with us?"

His face was darkening with anger, but she wasn't going to stop now.

"Don't you think it's hypocritical not to help the police? What would the media say if they found out you'd refused?"

"Don't you dare threaten me!" he shouted, and she saw that her baiting had pushed him past the point of fury. And the next moment, he did something Cami really hadn't expected.

His hand lashed out at her and caught her with a glancing blow on the side of the head.

With a cry of surprise, Cami reeled back, stumbling down on one knee.

And like a flash of lightning, Connor lunged forward, grabbed Rowan's arm, and jerked it down.

"You just assaulted a law enforcement officer. There weren't grounds to bring you in before this. But now, there are."

Rowan tried to yank his arm away. And the next moment, Cami gasped as he and Connor were actually grappling with each other. Rowan punched out and Connor ducked. Connor made a grab for his arm and Rowan wrenched away. With an angry yell, he kicked out and Connor staggered back. For a moment, she thought Rowan might actually get the upper hand. She heard fists thudding into flesh, the grunting and cursing as Rowan fought to take control. She stepped back hurriedly, feeling way out of her depth here and wanting to get away from this fight, because she didn't want another backhander like the one he'd given her. The whole side of her head was burning.

Then again, she might have to try and help if Rowan started beating up her investigation partner! She didn't want him to end up hurt.

But then, Connor dove forward, lashing out strongly. He got Rowan in a headlock, and they both staggered out onto the steps. Cami quickly retreated again, watching in growing anxiety, because this was seriously brutal. These guys were not playing. They were out to hurt each other, badly, and she had no idea what she could do, or how she could be effective, other than keeping out of their way. She really wasn't a fighter. She had no idea how Connor was managing to be so brutally effective. Now he was attacking Rowan, punching hard. Fists slammed into flesh.

Connor was still struggling to get the better of Rowan in this fight. Rowan had the weight advantage, and a rage and frustration that made him more dangerous.

Cami gasped as he wrenched away from Connor again, this time breaking free from his grasp.

But then Connor was on him again, grabbing his hands from behind, wrenching his arms behind his back, and slamming his shoulder into the door again so hard that the other man cried out in pain and rage.

With strength that shc hadn't expected, Connor flipped Rowan around, dropping him heavily to the driveway.

The other man's face was a mask of fury. He struggled and thrashed, but he couldn't break Connor's hold. Connor put a knee on his back and handcuffed him as Cami stared, wide-eyed and reluctantly admiring what it had taken to best this big, aggressive man in a one-on-one physical fight.

"You're under arrest. Now, you're coming with us, one way or another," Connor said, his voice firm and hard.

Rowan glared at him.

"You people have no idea who you're dealing with," he said, clearly furious. There was a distinct note of threat in his voice that chilled Cami. Suddenly, she wondered how Connor could sleep at night if he had to deal with these situations on a daily basis. Wasn't he scared someone might try and take revenge?

"We're dealing with a man who assaulted a law enforcement officer," Connor said. "That's already a crime. As for other offenses, that's what we're going to find out in questioning."

Grabbing the handcuffs, he shoved Rowan ahead of him, in the direction of the car.

***

Just fifteen minutes later, they walked into the closest police department in the suburbs close to where Rowan lived.

"It saves time," Connor muttered to Cami, as he escorted their suspect firmly into the lobby. "They always have space to spare."

Speaking to the officer at the front desk, Connor asked, "Do you have a room we can use?"

"Sure. You can use the interview room, first left, down the side passage," the officer said, seemingly unsurprised by the arrival of the FBI.

They headed down the passage and got Rowan into the interview room and on a chair.

The room was small and basic, with a wooden desk and three office chairs. In the room, Cami noted, it was strange how Rowan looked far less imposing a character than he'd done framed by the front door of his lavish mansion.

Now, under the harsh light, she could see that his skin looked dull, there was a scar on his right cheek, and his eyes were slightly reddened.

His expression was grim as he looked at them both.

"Now, Mr. Andrews," Connor said, getting straight to the point. "You're here because you assaulted a law enforcement officer. You're going to be charged with that, and we have sufficient cause to search your premises. Now, assuming you know your rights, you have the right to remain silent." He waited.

"You can't keep me here. I don't have to speak to you. I want my lawyer," he said, the words coming out in an angry growl. "I'm a very busy man, I have important meetings to attend. You're keeping me from doing my business for no good reason."

"Sure. Call your lawyer," Connor said. Cami guessed he couldn't refuse that request.

Rowan pulled out his phone and dialed a number. He spoke briefly.

"My lawyer's on the way. He'll be here in five minutes."

"We'll wait," Connor said.

The interview room was windowless. It felt a little claustrophobic. The air was cold. Cami watched as Connor passed the time by preparing. He made sure the recorder was working and took out a notepad. When Rowan had cut the call, Connor took his phone away and put it in a tray on the side of the room. He brought in a couple more chairs. All the while, Rowan watched him, with a baleful glare.

And then, a minor commotion in the lobby signaled that the lawyer had arrived. Not just one lawyer, Cami realized. A team of three lawyers. The legal task force trooped through with a clatter of footsteps. Three middle-aged men in expensive business suits. From their all-in-a-day's-work demeanor, Cami had the impression that they did a lot of work for Rowan.

"It's going to be crowded in here. You'd better go and observe," Connor told her.

Feeling sidelined but understanding that there really was a shortage of space in the room, Cami got up.

"Where do you want me to go?" she asked.

"Next door, there's a door with a window. Go watch through that, and you'll be able to hear everything," Connor said, pointing.

"I'll do that," she agreed.

"Take this with you for safekeeping." Connor gave her the tray containing Rowan's phone and car keys.

Carrying the tray, Cami quickly went out of the room, feeling the lawyers' stares pin her. They clearly had no idea who she was and were curious about her role.

Next door, she found another unoccupied interview room. There was a glass panel in the wall, and she could see the main interview room. Pressing her forehead against the cool glass, she could see Rowan, sitting at the table, flanked by the three lawyers.

On the other side of the table, Connor looked lonely by comparison. One agent against a wealthy, well-connected client and a strong legal team that looked like they'd done many rounds in this particular fighting ring.

Cami felt nervous about Connor's chances. How was he going to get information that could be used?

Would there even be a way?

And was there anything she might be able to do to help, behind the scenes?

Wondering how this would play out, Cami watched, fascinated, as Connor went strongly in for the attack.

CHAPTER EIGHTEEN

Cami pressed her face against the one-way glass, listening, fascinated, but also worried, as Connor began his interrogation. This seemed unfair to her. Why would one man need to lawyer up with such a huge team? Surely it indicated guilt, she wondered.

But Connor just went in strongly, not giving an inch to the bluster and threats of the three lawyers on the other side of the table.

"Release our client, now!" the lawyer to the right of the three pressured him.

Cami watched Rowan's expression. The other man's eyes grew colder, and his mouth turned down.

She thought he looked furious. But then, watching Connor, she realized that he was in his element. He was fighting back hard.

He spoke simply, effectively, and in a conversational tone, almost as if he was talking to a friend.

"Three women, who were playing Bordercross at the time, have been murdered within the past few days."

"That's unfortunate. But it's not our client's fault," the lawyer shot back.

As she listened to Connor start with the questioning, one man alone against a rank of lawyers and a defiant suspect, Cami realized something else. Something that could be important.

Rowan's phone was still lying in the tray.

Would it be possible to unlock it? It might not be necessary to hack. She'd seen the movement of his fingers earlier. She'd been watching closely in case he tried to pull any kind of stunt with that phone, being a high-profile IT expert. He hadn't done, but she remembered how his fingers had moved.

A zigzag with a tail.

Cami tried the same. A zigzag with a tail.

It didn't work, and she felt a thud of disappointment.

But maybe—maybe the tail had been longer. Maybe his finger had trailed down just one extra digit. Should she try again, or was she just heading for potential disaster here?

Knowing that three strikes meant she was out, Cami tried again.

The phone opened, and she huffed out a pleased and surprised breath. She'd done it! Immediately, she put it onto flight mode so that there could be no incoming calls, texts, or messages from this time onward. That way he wouldn't know that she'd been looking.

Connor was pressing on meanwhile.

"I need to know your whereabouts at the time of the deaths. The third victim was working on an expose of the company."

"You can't hold him for that. He didn't do it. There's no evidence. You can't keep him here!" the lawyer to the left of Rowan said. "You have no proof that this game is connected to these murders in any way. And if you try to say so publicly, we will sue you for damages."

"We want to know your client's whereabouts," Connor insisted.

With a sigh, the lawyer on the right said, "Give us the dates. We'll take a look at our client's calendar."

Connor pushed over a printed page and the legal team stared down.

"Our client was out of state on the second date. That is confirmable," the lawyer said. "We will provide you with that proof. We don't need to confirm the other dates. It's very clear the same person committed all these crimes. You need to release my client, now."

But what if he'd organized someone else to do it? As a hit?

Now that was a thought, Cami wondered. Connor clearly suspected the same.

"We are going to need your client's phone records, and also the bank details," he insisted. "There's too much at stake here not to need this information."

"You're accusing my client of having set this up?" the lawyer in the center asked, sounding outraged.

"We need to check out the possibility that you are behind the deaths." Connor spoke directly to his suspect.

Cami could see Rowan's mouth tighten. His gaze flicked around the room. He wasn't going to admit to anything, she realized. Most likely, even if he was innocent, he had other transactions that he was busy with and that he did not want the FBI knowing about.

"You know as well as I do what we are looking for," Connor said to the lawyers. "Evidence that your client hired someone to do this work for him."

"Why are you telling us this?" the lawyer pressured back. "We do not have to provide you with this information. My client has given you an alibi. Plus, you must understand, this is a huge corporation. He is not involved in the day-to-day workings of the game itself. He would have had no opportunity to do such a thing; he's not that hands-on. And if you think one journalist can bother him, you're wrong. He's had pieces written before. He always sues. That journo would have had her life destroyed by a lawsuit. That's how my client responds. Not by murdering. He doesn't need to do that."

"He would have had the expertise," Connor insisted. "He's an IT professional."

"My client works more on the visuals of the game, the big picture. Hundreds of developers, coders, and artists then do the rest of the work." The lawyer on the left folded his arms.

"Not all of them leave on good terms. We've dealt with defamation cases before. Disgruntled employees have challenged us and spread lies. This is nothing new to us," the lawyer in the center insisted. "You are very wrong to think this means anything to my client."

"And could those developers have contacted players after they quit? Accessed information?" Connor asked.

"Absolutely not! They sign a confidentiality agreement when they work for Virtual Ventures. And top-class security is in place. When every employee leaves, all the access passwords are changed immediately. Nobody would be able to hack into the game from outside. That is an absolute certainty."

Connor was pushing forward. "We want a list of everyone who has left your company, resigned, or been fired, in the last two years."

"Sure. We can give you that. Our client's HR department will provide that within a few hours. But you need to drop this harassment of him. We're not unreasonable. We will cooperate, of course. But we won't allow this bullying treatment from the police."

Cami realized that getting any information through either Rowan or the lawyers was going to be all but impossible. They seemed intent on putting the blame elsewhere. If Rowan himself was guilty, this was not going to be an easy task.

She didn't know if this would be allowed. Probably, it would not be allowed at all. She was sure Connor would shout her down big-time if she suggested it, but right now, Connor wasn't here. If she could access the phone's records, was there a possibility she could pick something up?

At least there would be some evidence then, and Connor would have a better idea of whether to pursue this suspect, or whether he could go on and explore other possibilities.

Quickly, she reached for the phone. What would be the best way? She guessed it would be to scroll through the records and simply film it with her own phone.

Cami found the list of recent calls and scrolled slowly through, allowing her phone to do the filming. Then, she scrolled through the texts.

Bank transactions would be more difficult. She couldn't get into his bank, not without risking creating message alerts and email alerts that he would know about, thanks to two-factor authentication. But that authentication would allow her to check another way, by reading through the messages the bank had sent. That she could do. She could film them all. That way even if one message had been deleted, there would be a gap that Connor could question.

Quickly, Cami accessed the bank messages and scrolled through, glad there was a record of those, too, filming them as well. There was a separate app where the crypto transactions were stored. Those could be useful she thought, taking screen shots. Crypto transactions were always a good way of paying when you didn't want it to go through official bank records.

"Our client needs his possessions back!" the lawyer threatened.

She'd only just been in time.

She hastily removed the phone from flight mode, then canceled the lock override. If she was quick, then maybe Rowan wouldn't even realize that anything had happened to his phone. She put her own phone away in her jacket pocket.

When Connor opened the door, Cami pushed the tray over to him.

We're going to need to keep you here while we confirm this alibi," he said. "Probably, another half an hour. Then we'll decide what to do about the assault charges."

"It had better not take too long," the lawyer threatened.

Connor walked out of the interview room.

"Connor," she whispered. "I don't know if it will help you, but while his phone was unlocked, I filmed the records. I thought maybe it would allow us to see if he'd been up to anything."

He stared at her in utter astonishment.

"You did what?" he said. "You know you're not supposed—"

At that point, he caught himself.

"That was good thinking," he said, still looking slightly shell shocked. "That could actually give us what we need. So, let's have a look, while my team confirms this alibi. If there is anything suspicious, we hold him. If not, we can avoid the trouble."

They hustled through to the back offices. Cami felt pleased and proud that her untoward idea might have been helpful, even if Connor was shocked by it.

"Read the numbers out to me and I'll run them through the system," Connor said.

"I also have bank transactions. Does anyone want to check those? And crypto transactions?" Cami asked. Since every minute counted, she guessed the more personnel that could work on them, the better.

"Yes. Forward those videos to this number." Connor read it out. "That's going back to the office. To Ethan, who's there now.

Cami pricked up her ears, feeling pleased that the likable Ethan would also be working on this pressured assignment. She sent the video through and then began reading out the numbers to Connor, who keyed them into the database, checking each one.

"There's nothing coming up in the calls. They all seem legitimate," he said, once she'd finished reading through the two-week record. "And let's see about the payments."

He got on the phone to Ethan.

"Anything stand out for you?" he asked. He raised his eyebrows. "Ah. Okay. Great."

Quickly, he disconnected.

"Nothing that raises alarm bells. A couple of strip clubs. A debt collection agency. But no large payments of the kind that indicate a hit has been paid for. So, I think we can rule him out. I'll hand him over to the local police. They can process the assault charges, so we can move on."

Cami let out a deep breath. After such an intensive search, after the fight to bring this suspect in, the answer wasn't here? It felt disappointing. It felt like a catastrophe. She'd thought she might have cracked the case by her sneaky capturing of the records.

It had all been for nothing, though. But Connor seemed to take it in his stride.

"We keep on looking, and keep on thinking," he said. "We go back to the case files. We review the information all over again."

Cami nodded. She guessed that was going to be the only way. And, as she thought back, another idea occurred to her.

"Perhaps this killer found the women via their IP addresses," she suggested. "Perhaps the IP addresses were visible to him, and he was able to access them in some way."

"What would that mean?" Connor asked her.

"Knowing an IP address would have allowed him to have gotten close by, if he was lucky and clever. But he would still have needed to search around for their exact location."

"He would have?" Connor asked, frowning.

"Yes. Maybe that would mean we could see him looking. Track his car license plate, or even catch sight of him, if there were cameras nearby any of the victims' homes."

Connor stared at her.

"What do you mean by all of that? What do you need?"

"Firstly, I'll need to check the case files of the earlier victims, to check if their IP addresses were visible and recorded while they played. I imagine that information would be in the case report, surely? I know the IP addresses themselves were there," she said. "Also, I don't know if I can do all this research on my phone. I'll need to use a laptop, to have multiple windows open."

Immediately, she saw Connor's face darken.

"I can't let you do that," he said. "Not now."

Anger flared inside her. This was her idea!

"Why not?" she asked. "Don't you trust me? There are lives at stake here. Please, trust me."

There was a long moment when he stared at her. Cami felt surprisingly anxious because Connor's reply meant a lot to her. Had his opinion of her changed?

She waited to see what his answer would be.

CHAPTER NINETEEN

Styx was hunting again. This was the part he enjoyed the most. The anonymity of the gaming world was refreshing. The spread of characters that he chose was intriguing. He didn't tie himself down to only one. Oh no, he was not that stupid.

He had a few different identities so that he could make sure to remain anonymous. It didn't matter who he was, his game personas were only part of the scenario.

But he knew to be careful because he didn't want to be caught. Staying ahead of the authorities, of that tall, dogged looking man in his FBI jacket and that strange, slim woman in the baseball cap—that was his aim now and it added another layer of challenge.

There were certain stipulations in place when he chose a victim. Certain parameters that ruled some out, even though they looked like attractive targets. But he had to stick to what was logically possible. He was, at heart, an extremely logical man.

And there was definitely no shortage. Not yet, although in time, he guessed he would need to move to another hunting ground, one of the other big cities, perhaps.

Moving into the game, he seamlessly blended into one of the crowded areas.

He was becoming extremely familiar with this game. Not only did he know its workings well, but he had played it for hundreds of hours now. He had taken his time with the first victims and planned his strategy very thoroughly.

Also, he was finding he took intense pleasure in the choosing. It was a thrill all on its own.

Within the game, as he mastered its complexities and got to know this alternative world, he was learning the best places to hide, the places to lurk and sneak up on a victim, out of sight.

The capture phase was what he liked best about this phase of the game. Capture was not a moment but rather a process. A long, exciting process of selection and discovery, and then of tracking, tracing, and planning.

It was an adrenaline rush from start to finish. His own version of Bordercross, he thought with a laugh, staring around his well-equipped study. His own, advanced version of the game.

Today, he was in the very heart of the game.

He was still in the inner city of this virtual world, but he'd left the cool, chic bars and clubs for the streets of a market. The stalls that were selling bright, colorful merchandise were leaping out at him with their bright pink strawberries, their shiny mangoes, and their green vegetables that were as fresh as if they'd been plucked from the ground this morning.

There were other areas in the game he enjoyed too. The concert venue had been where he'd targeted one of his victims, loving the way she'd danced.

His first one had been on the streets, walking in the public areas of the game, interacting with the other players. A friendly, sociable character—in the game, at least.

His third one had been more mysterious, someone who was more of a viewer and a watcher. She hadn't seemed to play actively in the game at all and in fact, had seemed a little out of sorts. But something about her had drawn him to her, and from that moment, with the other requirements in place, their meeting had been preordained.

Styx had mastered the ability to view a crowded area fast. He knew where he was going, and he wasn't hampered by the slow movements of the characters nor by the crowding of the market.

He was looking for names and avatars that appealed to him, that caught his eye. It gave him a thrill to think that their life or death might depend only on whether they were lucky enough—or, of course, unlucky enough—to attract his attention at exactly the right time.

He could be anyone. He could be anyone that he wanted to be.

He was looking for the most exciting and the most appealing victims. The ones who would make the game more interesting and make his victory more satisfying.

There was a flash of red hair.

He turned that way, instinctively, and saw a pretty girl with a body like a pin-up model. She was walking along, swinging her hips confidently.

But he'd had a confident victim. He wanted to push on, look for someone different, someone who was unlike the others. There was no point in repeating an experience. He wanted to push himself, seek what was new, seek what he knew would give him an even greater thrill.

This was the game. The reward was the capture. The pleasure was in the chase.

It was a game within a game. And he planned to play for a long time, judging from the number of victims he had left to choose from.

Like, for instance, the woman with the pink and white outfit, who was moving slowly through the crowd, one hand clutching a folder.

In the perfect chill of silence, he watched her from a distance, using his enhanced vision to get a better look.

This was a character that still had a grainy look to it, as if it hadn't been upgraded yet. He was sure she would do it soon when she realized the lack of capabilities that resulted from failing to upgrade. He smiled as he thought about what that upgrade would give him.

She had pale hair, cut in a bob like a 1940s movie star, with strands of it that kept escaping her cap and falling across her face. She was wearing pink lipstick, and from what Styx could see of her profile, she had a generous mouth with a wide lower lip.

Her eyes were large and deep set, with a serious, almost worried expression in them. It was clear that she was careful and cautious in her movements. It was clear she was likely to be an intriguing target.

He watched her a bit longer. Yes, she would do. She was an interesting choice. This girl was different. He couldn't see the details of her character, since it hadn't been upgraded, but he could see that her avatar had a flair for fashion and was very good looking.

He moved in closer to her. He wasn't sure if she was aware of him or not, but she didn't seem to be. He was fascinated by the way she moved.

He stayed focused on her, walking on her right, as he pretended to be busy looking at the fruit and vegetables in the stalls. He didn't act immediately. He watched her as she moved through the crowd. He waited until she was almost at the end of the lane, near to being out of sight.

He liked her name. BeachBaby.

Styx looked to see if he could learn anything more about this new target. He would need to check her account settings, to find out where she was based. He was looking for local players. That alone took a lot of narrowing down. But he'd already learned one of the secrets that could identify that quickly.

If she was local, which he would soon know, that would work perfectly. He would enjoy the drive. And in the more outlying areas, finding her would be easier.

Of course, living alone was also essential, and this was one point where a lot of the victims were ruled out when he did his real-life reconnaissance. He wanted single women. A boyfriend he could deal with, but a family made things too complicated. Plus, family women didn't get the time to play enough, and he needed to know that they would be absorbed in the game when he reached them for the final kill.

BeachBaby was the name a single girl would choose. Perhaps she lived in a house by the shore. She was very new to the game as well, he saw. That was good too. It meant she would be investing a lot of time in it. She was an enthusiastic new player and he liked those.

He was excited about her.

He made his way back to her, following her through the crowd.

It gave him a thrill to know that it was happening, that he was about to put the final stage in place before he revealed himself to her in real life.

He saw her avatar, now, at the end of the row, making her way out of the market. And at that moment, she came into clearer focus. She'd upgraded. She was now an integral person in the game and that meant he would know what he needed to.

And then, he let out a breath of disappointment as her character vanished from the screen. She'd gone, she'd left the game, and done so before he'd had a chance to get all the information he needed.

That was a bitter disappointment, but the ups and downs were all part of the experience.

Turning back to his screen, Styx forgot about this victim as he put BeachBaby out of his mind.

And he went hunting anew.

CHAPTER TWENTY

"No. I don't trust you."

Connor's words were a bombshell, and as he spoke, Cami felt tears flood her eyes. She couldn't believe it. Nothing she could do, no efforts she could make, would break through this man's distrust and dislike of her. Was he seriously going to put lives in jeopardy by blocking her from doing something that could help?

"It needs to be done! It can help the case! That's what I am focused on. The case! I have no interest in hacking your damned systems right now!"

Seething, Cami could see she still was not getting through to him. He either didn't believe she was telling the truth, or else he felt she'd bent the rules enough today already.

Spinning away, she stormed to the door.

"Do you want me to quit? Is that what you're trying to force me to do? Do the women's lives mean nothing?" she shouted.

She didn't care if jail awaited. She was going to fight for this, until he fired her, or she was forced to quit.

"That's not the situation," Connor countered. "Now calm down."

"Why?" Cami asked him, blinking the tears away, feeling angry he'd seen her moment of weakness. "How can I calm down when this investigation is at such a critical time? This can help us. It truly can."

Connor was silent.

He looked at her with a small bit of surprise, as if he hadn't expected to see her angry, as if he didn't expect her to be saying these things.

"You're not going to stay on the team for long if you continue this way," Connor said, his voice low and level. "If you quit, you're going straight to jail. It's your choice, but I'm not putting up with this juvenile acting out."

Cami stared at him. She had never felt so angry in her life. She wanted to grab the file from off of the shelf by the door and throw it at him.

"Juvenile?" Cami said, her voice rising. "What do you know about me? You only know the picture you have in your own mind. Is that how you think? That you can't even change your mind? No matter what I do? And this is what I'm doing now. I'm trying to make more of a difference. To help this case!" Cami felt her face flush. She didn't know who these words were coming from, only that they had seemed to rise up from the back of her mind and from the center of her soul.

"You don't respect our protocols. You can't even have a mature discussion on the subject. You think you have to have everything your own way," Connor shot back.

Cami was breathing hard. "You've always had these ideas about me. And you've never even tried to understand me. I've tried to do right by you, and this is the way you act? You're so arrogant! You think you're the only person in the world who knows how to do things!"

Cami felt like she was being railroaded. He was using his authority to bully her, to force her to obey. Flashbacks of her father's treatment surged in her mind, triggering her anger even more strongly.

"You've been assisting the FBI for less than twenty-four hours!" Connor argued. "You also need to prove yourself to earn other people's trust!"

"I am trying to prove myself by saving lives. And I've told you exactly how we can do it, and what I need to do to test this theory."

"You've requested unrestricted access to a very secure and privileged database. Maybe if you approached this in a different way, you would get a different result!"

"I don't know how to approach it any other way. I asked, and you said no. All you can do is say yes. If you won't say yes, then there's nothing further I can do. This is not a difficult choice! If you don't let me do what I need to do to save these women, I don't see how we can work together any longer! I don't want to work in a situation where I can't do what I need to do to help. Even if it means jail. I don't care. If you're not going to let me work, what else can I do? I have no option. I quit!"

In her frustration and passion, she was now blinded by tears. She hated this unfairness. She was getting flashbacks to her father's bullying. The sense of powerlessness was exactly the same.

Turning, she rushed out of the doorway, scrubbing her hands over her eyes as she headed along the corridor.

Seeing a restroom, Cami veered in and slammed the door. Turning on the tap in the small sink, she splashed her face.

This was so important to her now. More women might die. She recoiled from the thought of how someone could be innocently gaming, only to have a killer's hands roughly close around their neck.

She knew she shouldn't get so emotional, but she found it so difficult now that her heart was involved with the case.

Deep down, she knew that overreacting didn't help Connor. It didn't help solve the case. She guessed that it wasn't just about the confrontation between her and Connor. It was about her long-standing grudge with the FBI, her missing sister, her father's treatment, and the loneliness and rejection she had already experienced, too often, in life.

Cami turned away from the mirror, as memories of her father surged. His bullying ways. The domineering force he'd exerted over her. Jenna, her older sister by two years, had been the rebel who had stood up to him. She'd been the one who had tried to protect Cami from him, and mostly succeeded.

But then, Jenna had disappeared. Cami was certain she hadn't run away. She wouldn't have done that. No way would she have abandoned her younger sister that way. Something had happened, and rage surged in her all over again as she thought of her dad's token efforts to find her. He hadn't tried. Yes, he'd told her the FBI had gotten involved, but she'd never heard more. It seemed there was no more to be heard. They hadn't tried hard enough, either.

She was all alone, and she might as well get used to it, Cami thought, trying to harden her heart against the onslaught of emotion that threatened to overpower her.

She couldn't help that it was a secure database. All she wanted was to help the women. Surely there was a way to do that, without being blocked at every turn? Why hadn't he suggested something himself? He knew what the possibilities were.

Then a terrible thought came to her.

Had she imagined that she and Connor were getting closer, and were starting to feel as if they were working together? Had he been waiting for this moment, for her to resist him and to rebel against the rules, so that he could do what he'd been wanting to all along, and send her to jail?

The possibility flared in her mind, a scary and unwanted thought. She didn't want to believe that of Connor. But then, she'd never believed that the FBI would have failed to find her sister.

There were terrible truths in life that had to be accepted, and a lot of them depended on people you wanted to trust.

And, at that moment, there was a hard, loud knocking on the restroom door.

"Cami Lark?" a woman's voice sounded, sharp and officious. "Jacenta Jones here, FBI. Are you done in there? I need to meet with you."

This was it. Her fate was sealed. There could only be one reason for a head office visit at this time.

With her heart in her boots, Cami unlocked the door and stepped out, gathering the courage she needed for what she knew would happen next.

CHAPTER TWENTY ONE

This was it, Cami thought. She felt a sense of deep regret that she'd been so impulsive, so thoughtless in her decision making. She'd been so triggered by Connor's hard reluctance to let her go ahead with her idea, knowing that lives could be saved, that she'd lost her temper. She could have handled the whole situation better, but he'd gotten under her skin too deeply, and she hadn't been able to regroup and retry.

She stepped outside, looking in surprise at the woman waiting there.

Jacenta was a tall, regal looking woman with raven-black hair and large, dark eyes. Her hair was coiled around her head in a tight, neat bun, and she wore a blue skirt and crisp white blouse. She had an imposing and forceful demeanor. She stared at Cami and immediately, Cami sensed this woman didn't like her much. There was disapproval in her gaze. But that didn't matter. It would probably make her job easier, in fact, given what she was here to do.

"I need to speak to you in private, Ms. Lark. Come with me," Jacenta commanded. "We'll find an open meeting room and get this done."

Get it done? Cami's stomach twisted.

Clearly familiar with the police department's layout, Jacenta headed to her left, power walking down the corridor with Cami hurrying behind.

There was no time for anything. No time for preparation, for excuses. She'd brought this on herself, after all. A minute later, Jacenta had reached one of the meeting rooms, tapped on the door, and finding it empty, opened it, and led the way inside.

Cami followed her in. Jacenta closed the door.

The meeting room had a window overlooking the back parking lot, and a small, square table with six chairs. Rain was still spattering the window. The overhead light looked harsh and bright.

Jacenta indicated a chair on the opposite side and Cami sat. Meanwhile, Jacenta placed her briefcase on the desk and opened it, taking out a folder and a few documents.

Then she sat, and for a moment, she didn't say a word. She simply stared at Cami, who felt as if she was going down in an elevator too quickly. That was the sensation she had as she stared back. Her mouth dry and her heart racing, she waited for what was to come, feeling as if she was trapped inside a slow-motion nightmare.

"I'm from the Boston office. I have been briefed on your background situation," Jacenta continued.

Cami nodded miserably.

Jacenta put a hand to her chin, and Cami felt as if she was being sized up. "I've been given the background to the reasons you attempted to breach our system. And I've been apprised of the conditions you were given, the deal you were offered as an alternative to jail."

"Understood," Cami said, her stomach churning.

"The FBI feels you have potential, you possess skills they need, and that's why you received the offer of being co-opted onto the team for this case. But they still recognize that your behavior and character is very out of line. Until this case is closed, you still have the alternative of a prison sentence, and that's a reality. So, for this time, the FBI is considering you as a paroled offender. And I am your probation officer."

"What?" Cami said incredulously.

This was turning out to be totally different than she'd thought. This scary official was not, in fact, here to escort her to prison. She was having a probationary hearing. Something she hadn't dreamed would happen.

"You committed a felony," Jacenta said sternly. "What you did was very serious, and I think you know that. But, if you comply with our conditions and show good behavior, the matter will be closed. Your liberty will be restored. And I'm here to provide you with any guidance you need to make sure you keep on the right path while you're working with the FBI. I have a psychology and social work background, and I'm here to support and advise you."

Cami shook her head. She still felt utterly blindsided by this. Jacenta herself was a scary character, she thought. She could see the woman didn't like her as a person. Most probably she held her in contempt, the way a law enforcement officer might perceive a criminal. She didn't know what support she could possibly provide.

"I don't know what to say," she said. "I think I've already messed up too badly."

"Why's that?" Jacenta asked.

"Because I had an argument with Connor just now. It was a bad one. I said I was quitting."

Jacenta nodded. "Yes. He mentioned that when I arrived. He said he'd talk it through with you when I leave."

"He did?" This meeting was providing one shock after another, Cami thought. She'd have imagined Connor would have been baying for her blood. There was a chance for her?

Feeling less edgy now, she listened as Jacenta continued.

"Let's get one thing straight," her probation officer said stiffly. "You were co-opted by the FBI because they believe you have the potential to help with a technical, complex case. That's the whole point of why I'm here. But, if you breach their trust, you will end up in prison. Do you understand that? You've been given a second chance. Now, you have to prove you're worthy of that trust."

"But…but this whole argument happened because Connor doesn't trust me," Cami tried. "There was something important I wanted to do, and he wouldn't allow me access."

Jacenta stared at her. "And you couldn't find a way around that? A way of working together with him? One thing I should tell you is that the FBI puts great emphasis on working in a cooperative environment. And it's up to you to create that. Nobody is going to do it for you. So, if you don't have those skills, you need to learn them. Fast."

Cami met her gaze. She knew she was being judged and tested. She knew she would be judged harshly if she failed. But she did not feel she was in a good position to comply.

"You live with the choices you make," Jacenta reminded her.

"Look," she said after a moment, struggling to keep her voice steady, "I know what I did was wrong and criminal. The hacking, I mean. I understand that. But I get so frustrated with the bureaucracy. The red tape. Years ago, my sister went missing, and she was never found. I know the FBI was involved in the case, but nothing happened. I feel as if they failed me and failed her too. That's why I get so frustrated when I can't do what I need to. It takes me right back to the way I felt then. It makes me worried that this will end up going the same way."

"I'm sorry about your sister. There may be more to it, and if you speak to Connor at a later stage, perhaps he can look it up and give you the details."

Cami nodded. She didn't know if speaking to Connor again was in her future at all. It might be too late for that already. But if it wasn't, she resolved to try.

"And I understand you feel you've been caught in this situation, Ms. Lark," Jacenta said calmly. "But, listen to me, and listen carefully. The rules and red tape that you feel so frustrated by are in place for a reason. It's because the FBI has to work within the framework of the law, and if they don't, then a case can fall apart. And that's a disaster beyond our powers to fix. So, things have to be done correctly."

Cami nodded. "I'm not good at following rules. I know," she said humbly.

"So far, your reports from Agent Connor have not been negative. There have been a few issues mentioned, but nothing serious."

"Is that so?" Cami asked, feeling surprised.

"That's correct." Jacenta continued in a businesslike tone. "Now, we don't have much time. I know this case is putting you under a lot of pressure. And I hope I've given you some guidance on your current issue. Now, I need to know, firstly, if you have everything you need to do your job. Is there anything you require? Any problems you have come up against that you want to speak about?"

Cami thought.

"I guess I have everything I need for now. If…if I'm doing this full time, or regularly, from here on, I can bring my laptop. That's still in my room at the university residence and I haven't been back there since. I'd like it in the future. I'm okay for everything else. I bought a few fresh clothes. I don't actually need that much." She smiled ruefully.

To her surprise, Jacenta nodded, showing the first faint flicker of approval Cami had seen.

"That's probably an advantage when teamed up with the FBI. Everyone is on the move all the time." She tapped her fingers on the desk. "Then, here's my number. If you have any issues, if anything is bothering you, call me." She handed over a business card. "Talk if you need to. Call me if there are issues. Most times, you'll find they can be solved without the need for escalation or fights. Or hacking attempts. Or trying to quit."

She stared at Cami, stern again. Cami felt herself redden.

"Thank you. I will."

And, at that moment, the interview room door opened. Connor stood there, his face grim.

Cami took a deep breath. Time to apologize.

CHAPTER TWENTY TWO

Cami knew she needed to show Connor, and Jacenta, that she could act with a cool mind, and in the cooperative way that Jacenta had put such emphasis on.

"I'm sorry, Connor. I overreacted. I understand the databases are privileged. Is there a different way we can do this? Would you let me take a look under supervision? Or could I just instruct another agent on what to do?"

She waited, holding her breath, and felt a flare of relief when he nodded.

"Let's put what happened aside, and get moving on this," he said. "We don't have time to waste. We need whatever information we can get because this case is now critical. I checked the history. The victims did use IP addresses. So now, we need to work remotely with Ethan, to look for footage, and track this guy down."

Hustling to the back office with him again, Cami felt as if things were moving forward. There was an atmosphere of excitement and tension in the office, and Ethan was already on speaker phone.

Since the victims had logged in using IP addresses, the killer could very well have gotten their approximate location by using those. Now, Ethan was busy checking if there was camera footage near any of their homes that could be used to catch sight of him as he'd tried to pinpoint their location physically.

"There's nothing near Kate Warner's place," Ethan said, sounding disappointed.

"And the others?" Cami asked.

"Yes. I'm picking up a few traffic cameras and security cameras in the apartment lobby, which will also help us. That footage will be fairly quick to obtain. I'll work on it immediately."

"While you get that done, I need Cami this side," Connor said. She turned to him.

"I'm going to show you how to access the case archives. I've cleared it with Fraser. You may need to get into historic cases from time to time, so it's right that you have permission. We've created a guest passcode you can use," he said. "Bear in mind it is traceable. Your movements within the system will all be visible to other users."

Cami felt astounded and pleased that he was giving her this access.

Had she managed to prove herself to him at last? He wouldn't have changed his mind about that unless he'd decided he could trust her. Not Connor, whose thinking had felt as if it was set on railroad tracks, unchangeable and cast in steel.

She felt proud that she'd managed to get over herself, to show that she could work together with him. She was pleased that she had the permission to do this. And more than that, she felt surprisingly pleased, as if a conflict point that could have destroyed things, had been worked through.

Moving over to the computer as Cami scooted onto the chair, Connor showed her how to log into the FBI databases and access the case archives. It was a fairly simple step by step process, requiring a couple of passwords and authentication along the way.

"Thanks for the information," she said, turning to the screen again and running through the protocols once more so she was sure of them.

Connor got on the phone again and began speaking rapidly to Ethan.

"The first footage should be coming through in a moment," he told her.

As she sat by the computer, waiting for the footage, Cami turned the angles of the case over and over in her mind, looking for other ways, other possibilities that could be used to track him down.

She took another look at all the player avatars in the case files. How was he choosing them, she wondered. What were his parameters? For a start, he seemed to be killing only in Boston, but the gamers were from all over the country and the world. So that alone would mean that he spent a lot of time narrowing down his potential killing field. And again, it would point to good IT knowledge and the ability to do research. How did he know where they were from? IP addresses only?

He was also a gamer. That was obvious. He knew his way around the game and how to use it for his purposes. So, that meant he was someone who played often. Cami had no doubt he was highly intelligent. He had to be.

"We're starting to get information," Connor said, interrupting her thoughts. "We got lucky on this. Adriana's neighborhood has cameras at every intersection, and they are forwarding that footage now. With a camera at each end of her street, and on the corner, it would pick up for sure if a car was driving up and down, looking to locate a certain IP address."

"That sounds good," Cami said.

"And Liz Hughes's apartment block has a camera in the lobby, and also one outside. The footage outside doesn't cover the entire street, but maybe we can get lucky."

"He might have scoped it out earlier and come back. If I had been him—I've been trying to put myself into his mindset—that's what I would have done," Cami said. "I would have located the person first, knowing it might take time. And then, when they were playing online the next time, it would be easy to come back again."

Connor narrowed his eyes thoughtfully.

"Yes. That makes sense. Too risky to do everything in one go, especially since two of the kills took place in the evening, when traffic would have been lighter and if a car had been driving up and down, it might have been noticed."

"So, we are looking for a vehicle, or a person, that came in twice. He could have come in his own car, or a rented car, or even taken a cab though. It depends how carefully he was looking to cover his tracks."

Cami frowned. This was definitely a complex issue.

"You couldn't drive up and down in a cab, though. So even if he was walking, he'd be visible."

"Let's see what the footage gives us."

He turned one of the laptops in her direction. "I'll screen share so we can both look."

While she waited for it to download, Cami thought again of what Jacenta had said. Connor had had a few issues but no major complaints. That was surprising to her. Maybe Connor was being harsh on her now, but not being unfair.

Maybe there was a possibility that they could work together. Maybe, in partnership, they could solve this case.

There was the footage, coming through now. Cami looked at the images appearing on the screen, feeling slightly worried by the graininess. She was going to have to focus hard on this in order to get the details.

But as she watched the footage, her eyes adjusted, and she found it easier to pick up what she was looking for. First, the date stamp. The footage was available from a week before the murders, going forward, which Cami thought was a sensible timeline.

First prize would be the same car in both locations.

But the amount of footage was absolutely mind numbing. This was going to take hours. Days, in fact, and there was going to be a high proportion of risk for human error, especially as the hours went past.

"Is there a program that can check this?" she asked.

Connor frowned. "When it's something like this, no. The vehicle surveillance companies have plate recognition, but for something like this, with two different sets of footage, no. We do it the hard way, the old-fashioned way. It ends up being quicker," he sighed.

But Cami was thinking.

She'd written a program similar to this last year. It had not been identical, but it had been close enough that she thought she could adjust it. With a few tweaks, the visual recognition program she'd put in place might be able to do the job. At any rate, Cami decided, she'd rather spend half an hour seeing if she could customize it, than spend easily the whole day staring at this footage. There were cars the whole time!

"There's something I have here, a plate recognition program, that might be able to be adapted," she said. She felt nervous suggesting it. After the way her last idea had gone down, she didn't have a clue whether he would agree to doing it, or whether she'd be shot down in flames all over again.

CHAPTER TWENTY THREE

Cami saw Connor look up, surprise on his face at her suggestion, and for the first time, she saw actual hope in his eyes.

"A number plate recognition program?" he asked.

"Yes. I wrote it for something else, as a college test. But I think it could be customized in order to fit in with what we have here."

"Now that would be a real time saver," Connor said, and she now saw he hated this mind numbingly tedious checking just as much as she did.

"Where can I run it?" she asked, hesitant to upload a new program onto an actual police machine. She thought that might set off alarm bells, either figurative or literal. "I mean, I don't want to get into trouble, Connor. But it can't run off my phone, and it'll have to be uploaded somewhere."

There was a short pause.

Then, with a sigh, Connor pushed over his own machine to her. The police laptop she'd been using, he turned in his own direction.

"Here you are," he said.

"Thanks," Cami said, feeling surprisingly grateful for the trust he'd shown. That truly was trust, right? Giving her his personal machine so that she could run an experimental program on it had to be a sign of trust.

She turned Connor's laptop in her direction, aware that it was older and a slower machine—by her standards—and that she could not risk compromising it in any way. She would have to be careful and considerate of its user, who must have a wealth of important data stored on here.

Going online, she found her program and installed it. The program loaded. She checked it over for a moment. It was a pretty simple visual recognition program. As her lecturer for that class had repeatedly told her—for goodness' sake, keep it simple. Now, Cami was grateful all over again for this advice.

Then she started making the changes she'd need to do for it to pick up the points of similarity in between the two sets of footage—with room for yet another comparison point to be added if they obtained the third set.

It was easy to tweak the program, and she was feeling optimistic by the time she'd put in the basic parameters.

Next, she started the process of capturing the footage, and waited as the lines of text began to churn across the screen, scrolling down, faster and faster. The program was working, just like it was supposed to.

She hit play, and let the footage run.

"Coffee?" she asked.

Connor looked up, surprised. "Sure," he said. "Thanks."

Cami went to the kitchenette she'd blasted past earlier, in a temper and needing to get away. There was a jug of coffee there and she poured two cups, put sugar and cream on the tray, and took it through. There was no point in watching while the program ran. It wouldn't make it go any faster. In fact, she'd always felt it was better luck to walk away.

She took the tray back, passed Connor his cup, took one of her own, and then returned to the screen.

Immediately, she saw something there.

"Connor!" she said. "It's got a match."

He jumped up and hurried around to look. "Already?"

"Yes. There might be more, but this is the first, clear one. It's a black vehicle and it has out-of-state plates. Virginia plates."

"That's excellent." He was looking at her with something she was sure was respect. Then he scanned the time stamps for the camera footage.

"It was in each of the two locations the day before the murders. That's close enough to mean something. Let's look up those plates."

Connor logged into the FBI database from the police computer because Cami's program was still running on his own machine.

"It's worth checking this out, even if there are others, if he's been here for the duration of all these murders. He could have traveled here to commit the crimes, and then be planning to go back home or else hit another city," Connor said.

He waited for the database to process the information.

"Okay," he said. "The vehicle is licensed to a man called Francois Leeming. I'm going to see what we can find out about him. And while we do that, I'm getting an urgent APB out on the vehicle. We need to know where he is now."

Hurriedly, Connor called the office, and instructed them to get the APB out as urgently as possible.

Then, he returned his focus to the screen. Feeling as impatient as he now looked, Cami hurried around to peer at it and learn more about this suspect.

There was Francois's ID pic. He looked to be in his thirties—which a moment later, his date of birth confirmed. He was thirty-two.

"He works in IT," Cami said, surprised, as that information flashed up. "That would have allowed him to track those IP addresses. So, that's a definite connection. I see he's a programmer who's currently freelancing."

"Yes. If he's in that industry, it makes sense that he would have had that knowledge," Connor agreed.

Cami felt filled with excitement. The suspect they needed could be here. Right here. Now all they needed to know was where he was. Where was he driving now in that sleek, black car? Having out of state plates would at least make him easier to spot.

She wished she could tune in to his mind. But in a way, Cami guessed she'd already been trying to do that. She'd been doing her best to think like the killer, and by doing so, they'd uncovered this suspect.

If he was trawling for new victims, he might be out and about now. She imagined him, driving up and down the road where his research took him next, using whatever software and intelligence he had available to narrow down the location of the next woman he planned to kill.

That was a very scary thought, especially seeing all they could do now was sit here. As of a few minutes ago, every police officer was now apprised of the number plate and knew that it was urgent. But if he wasn't on the move at all, the plate wouldn't be spotted. So many factors had to coincide. He had to be out on the road, in view of a police vehicle, or else recorded by a police camera that was monitored and checked.

Cami wished it didn't feel so much like hunting a needle in a haystack.

She returned to her chair, sipping on her coffee, watching her program at work as it sorted through the footage. Perhaps they would get other hits. This was their first, and also the most recent comparison, but the program was working back through the footage and there might be others. She tried to curb her impatience. She didn't want to wait for others. She wanted to go out, now, and hunt for this suspect. She wanted to know why Francois Leeming had driven all the way from Virginia, to spend the last few days right here in Boston, with footage recorded near two of the victims' homes so far.

And then, Connor's phone range. He drew in his breath triumphantly.

"There's a hit on the vehicle. A security roadblock just outside town said it appeared on their footage ten minutes ago, on the highway into downtown. Let's get moving. I'm going to ask for all available cars in the area to join us. He's on that road and moving into town. If we're fast, we might be able to find him."

CHAPTER TWENTY FOUR

Cami ran out, behind Connor, feeling resolute as they chased after their latest, strong suspect who was in IT and who had been in the vicinity of both victims' homes a day before the crimes.

This might be a chase-down. She'd never been involved in those before. And, as Connor jumped into his car, pulling off at high speeds before Cami had even gotten her seatbelt on, she knew this was going to be totally different from what she'd ever dreamed she'd be doing in this job.

She struggled to do up her belt, nearly slewing sideways as Connor sped away, driving totally differently from the way he usually did. The car whipped around a corner. The radio was crackling, and they were flying along on the main road in the fast lane.

Connor was on the radio, communicating with the other teams on the road, and putting the word out for other available cops to join them.

Cami couldn't make out everything that was being said. Her ears weren't tuned to the sounds of the radio or to the lingo that they used in their communication.

"We've located the suspect's car."

That one, she did hear clearly, with a jolt of excitement. Someone ahead was on track to stop Francois Leeming.

"Flagging him down. Requesting him to stop."

The voice on the radio sounded so routine, as if stopping a suspected criminal for questioning was all in a day's work. Cami guessed it was.

But then, the voice spoke again, this time with a note of panic, and clearly enough for her to hear.

"Suspect has failed to stop! He's made an illegal turn and is now heading down the slip road to the highway. We have to backtrack."

"We're on it!" Connor said.

Cami thought they had been in a chase before now. She realized she'd been wrong as Connor hit the gas, hard, and activated the siren.

The car flew down the main road and the view seemed to telescope ahead of them as he sped up. And then, reacting to something indiscernible he heard in the radio feed, he hit the brakes, slewing it sideways, speeding down another slip road. Cami's heart jolted in time with the wheels as she felt the magnitude of the situation. This was truly last-moment decision making. What if they missed him?

Now they were on the highway itself, racing at a furious speed.

"We might need to be ready to make a turn. We're going the opposite way to him. Approaching where his vehicle should be," he said in a clipped voice.

Cami nodded, trying to ignore the way her stomach was skipping, and her heart was beating like a drum. It was all she could do to stop herself from grabbing the dash as Connor hit the brakes, swearing, when another car veered into their path.

"What are we going to do if we do locate it?"

"Stop it. If we can, without risking the lives of any civilians."

Cami kept her eyes on their surroundings, as Connor checked and changed lanes, speeding along at a furious rate. Where was the black BMW with Virginia plates? Would they see it suddenly, in this busy lunch time traffic, and if so, would they be able to catch up? The way Connor was driving, Cami thought that would be likely.

The radio crackled, and Connor replied, his voice urgent.

"Copy that. We're turning."

Cami gasped as he hit the brakes, screaming practically to a stop in the fast lane, before veering sideways across the highway. Now, she really did clutch at the seat as the car sped the opposite way, accelerating furiously in the fast lane heading south, as horns blared and traffic swerved around them.

It would have been exciting if it wasn't so scary. This was no video game, this was real life, and Cami felt acutely aware of the risks Connor was taking. Calculated risks to be sure, but even so, chasing down a criminal was a next-level adrenaline rush. And they wouldn't stop until they caught this man. They couldn't. But where was he?

Cami heard the voice of the officer they'd dispatched to follow-up the location of the vehicle. The one who was now collating information from various cameras and reports.

"It's heading in the same direction as you. On the same road."

Ahead, she could see the cars all pulling to the left, onto the slip road. The last of them was a black one.

Cami felt her heart leap as she saw it, even at that distance.

"We've got it!" shc said, breathless. "We've got it."

Connor called into the radio. “We’ve got visual on the vehicle. Requesting all units report in to block the road ahead.”

“Copy that,” came the reply.

Cami’s heart was pounding. This was it. This was the end of the chase. They were about to catch him. She craned her neck, trying to get a closer look at the car. Behind them, the sound of more sirens sounded.

Connor swerved into the fast lane, passing the cars that were already merging onto the slip road.

“We can’t lose him now!” he said. “I’m going to get ahead of him, and then force him to stop, if I can. If I can,” he added in frustration because the lights were changing.

He hit the brakes, hard, and Cami yelled in alarm.

Cars swerved around them, sounding their horns, but Connor kept them on the road, speeding towards the traffic light they were approaching.

The light turned red. Connor, who she hoped had been through enough moments like this to know what he was doing, didn’t slow down.

“We’re going through!” Cami exclaimed, aghast. Horns blared and the siren screamed as they accelerated through the red light. Cami closed her eyes as an oncoming car hit the brakes, slewing to the side.

Then she opened them again because there was no way she could keep them closed. Not when they were catching a suspected killer.

They were through the intersection, miraculously undamaged. And they were speeding toward the car ahead. But Francois Leeming wasn’t slowing down. If anything, he was increasing his speed. He surely had a reason for trying to run? A guilty reason?

Going at least thirty miles over the limit, they sped toward the intersection. Cami was willing the traffic lights to stay green, because she couldn’t take another near-miss experience like the one she’d just had.

Connor sped through the intersection, with a screech of tires, and Cami held her breath, her knuckles gripping the seat, her heart beating in her ears.

They were gaining on the black car ahead of them, but Cami guessed it was going at least a hundred miles an hour, even at this stage, and was showing no sign of slowing.

“Can we force him to stop?” she asked, her voice eager. Surely, they couldn’t let this criminal get away now.

"We will if we can," he said grimly.

The radio crackled.

"He's turning off the main road. He's taking evasive action again."

Connor swore. "He's heading into a residential area. That's the last thing we need, the way he's driving."

"Get around. He's heading for Plumtree Road. That connects with South. If you can get onto South, you can cut him off."

"Copy," the voice came back.

Connor swore again, and switched lanes, speeding past cars that were suddenly braking and swerving out of their way.

Taking the side road, he turned off the main road and onto South. Now, Cami's heart was in her mouth. The BMW was starting to pull away from them, and if backup didn't close in from the other side, it was going to be all over.

"Looks like he's turning," Connor said.

Cami peered forward and saw the black car, with its distinctive license plates, turning off into a residential street.

Connor followed, swerving around the corner, tires screeching. But they were closer now.

And then, ahead, with a rush of triumph, she saw another police car, oncoming, swerving diagonally to block the road so that the BMW hit the brakes, wheels smoking. He was trapped.

Two officers jumped out of the police car and pointed their guns at the driver. With a shock, Cami realized that one of the men was Ethan. She recognized him as they pulled up, slewing into position behind the car, trapping it in between the two police vehicles.

"Stay put. Stay here," he said, sounding as breathless as she felt. She was only too glad to watch as this armed showdown played out. Now holding his own firearm, Connor got out and approached the car.

"Francois Leeming," he shouted. "Get out of the vehicle. Hands in the air."

Cami waited, holding her breath, watching Ethan as he advanced, holding his weapon. His face looked intent, but Cami wondered if Ethan felt scared at these times, as a new agent. He couldn't have had much experience in a real, live scene like this. She knew it was beyond anything she'd ever imagined.

Would Francois get out willingly? Would he try and fight back?

She felt relieved for her team members as she saw him step out of the car and got her first real-life sight of him—a slim looking, brown-haired man, wearing a dark jacket and shades. He looked about five-ten. His shoulders were broad. She wondered if he fitted the strangler's description of "average strength." He looked angry but intimidated.

At least he wasn't going to shoot them, Cami thought. But as Ethan and Connor stepped forward to handcuff him, Cami knew that this was only one step of the way. Now they needed to question him, look for an alibi, or prove his guilt.

And, as an IT expert, she had the feeling that like his driving, he would have a whole stack of evasive maneuvers ready to unleash.

CHAPTER TWENTY FIVE

While being processed, Francois Leeming had not requested a lawyer. He hadn't requested anything. He'd remained utterly silent. Now, Cami waited expectantly outside the door of an interview room at the FBI Boston office to see how the confrontation with this suspect would play out.

This time, thanks to the absence of any legal team so far, she was pleased that she could stay in the room for the questioning. Even so, she didn't think that this was going to be easy. Not at all. She guessed this was going to be their toughest suspect in this case so far.

Connor opened the door, nodding at Cami, who walked in behind him. Looking at Leeming now, seated at the table, Cami sensed this man had something to hide. She didn't consider herself an expert in body language at all. But even as a lay person, she could see how closed up he was. His eyes were narrowed. His shoulders tight. His fingers closely laced.

He was not going to give anything up. Immediately, she saw this. But she was just a beginner in this game and perhaps Connor could blast through his defenses.

It was perturbing to Cami, though, that he'd refused to open his laptop or to unlock his phone. He'd just outright refused when he was being processed. They were going to ask him about that again now, but she had a feeling he was locked up as tight as his devices clearly were.

Connor sat down at the table and started the recorder. Francois Leeming looked at Cami. He sneered, and Cami found herself feeling angry.

"We're questioning you in connection with a series of murders in the Boston area," Connor told him in a neutral voice.

Leeming simply shrugged. "Why me? I have nothing to do with any murders," he said.

He didn't even seem shocked or surprised, Cami noted, now feeling even more suspicious. Wouldn't anyone be shocked if they were confronted with this information?

Connor simply continued. "Your car was seen in the vicinity of two of the crimes, twenty-four hours before they were committed."

"Well, where were the murders? You'll have to tell me as I don't know. I know nothing. I've been driving around town, sure. There's a chance I could have been in the same area, sure. Even if I was, it's not proof of anything. So, it could only have been a coincidence, right? That I was in that place at that time?" Leeming insisted.

Cami looked at his face. His eyes were narrowed in a way that was, to her at least, suspicious. He was hiding something.

"What is your purpose for being in Boston?" Connor asked.

"I'm here on business."

"Can you prove that? Where are you staying?"

"The Hyatt. Near the harbor."

"For how long are you checked in?"

"I arrived last week. I'm checking out in a couple of days."

"Can you prove you are here on business?"

Leeming folded his arms. "I'm an IT developer. My business here is confidential. I don't disclose what clients I see or what I discuss. I'm one of the best in the business and if they call me out to brainstorm some possibilities, I don't say why. Not before or after the contract is signed."

Cami thought that was a rather egotistical thing to say. She was surprised by it. She would have thought that a truly professional developer probably would not have bragged that way. Developers didn't have to claim they were the best in the business. That was more the domain of the salespeople, in her experience.

There was a long pause. Cami felt him watching her again and looked up. Their gazes clashed. He looked at her steadily, smirking. Cami looked away. She did not like him. She didn't like him at all.

"Why was your car seen near the crime scenes?" Connor asked again.

"I don't know. Clearly, I was in the area."

"Can you tell me who your clients are?"

"No. Not until they sign." There was a pause. "This doesn't make me a killer, does it?"

"What is your business here?"

"That's confidential. I'm not telling you that. If I don't sign a contract, then I don't tell. That's how it works. I'm not giving any details about my work."

"Can you prove you're here for work?"

Leeming paused for a moment.

"You're going in circles here. I'm not proving anything. I don't have to. You have no evidence to state otherwise."

"Open your phone." Connor passed him the device.

"I can't do that."

"Why not?"

"I don't recall how. It's a new phone."

"How are you doing business then?"

He shrugged, looking smug and secretive. "I was on my way to the store to get it unlocked."

Cami shook her head at this blatant lie. This was just making a mockery of the questioning. He was not even trying to give a plausible story but was simply throwing back insulting ideas.

"We don't believe you," Connor said.

"Prove me wrong," Leeming countered.

Cami tensed. She knew it was going to be hard to prove anything when the man was so cagey.

"What was your real purpose for being in the area where the crimes occurred?" Connor asked.

"I'm not telling you that. That's confidential work."

"Open your laptop," Connor ordered.

"I can't do that," Leeming said.

"Why not?"

"There's a password."

"Open it."

Leeming shook his head.

"I can't do that. I don't recall the password."

There was a flicker of a smile on his face. Cami's eyes narrowed. She knew that smile. She'd seen it before. It was the look of someone who was lying. Of someone who was bluffing. Of someone who had something to hide.

"What was your purpose for being in the area of the crime scenes at those specific times?"

"I'm not answering that."

"Can you tell me who you're here to see?"

"No."

"We'll get what we need," Connor told him. He gestured to Cami. "We have sufficient cause to seize these devices. We'll open this laptop. And your phone too. We'll get what we need. But if you do it willingly, at least you're cooperating. If you're not cooperating, it means you have something to hide."

"Unfortunately, I'm very aware of security. My devices are highly secure. You won't find a way into them. The encryption is state of the art. It's not something you can get into; not fast, anyway."

He spoke with confidence that made Cami feel nervous. She didn't think he was bluffing about this. She thought he was telling the truth. His devices were highly encrypted. She was sure she could get past the security levels, but it would take time.

She cleared her throat, wondering if she could contribute to this discussion. If she pressed his buttons, perhaps he would flare up and they'd learn something by how he replied in anger.

"Okay. I am going to tell you now. I don't believe you're such a hot IT specialist," she said dismissively. "I don't think you have the ability to do what you're saying. I think you're bragging too much and you're just all talk. Forgetting a password? Seriously? I mean, who does that?"

As she'd hoped, that got to him. Having a young woman criticize him was clearly something that rankled.

"I am the best in the business. I don't have to brag about it," he said angrily, his eyes narrowed.

"But you've just been bragging about it," Cami pointed out.

"What is your point?" he flashed back at her.

"My point is that I don't think you were at these places coincidentally. And I'm sure that if we opened your devices, we'll find proof of that," Cami said. "That's why you don't want us looking, isn't it? Because we'll find something incriminating. Maybe a map pin drop, maybe a message, maybe a record of their real addresses or their IP address. Prove me wrong!" she challenged.

He hissed in a frustrated breath.

"Okay, if you want to know, I…I did know Adriana Knight, who was killed. I heard about her murder. I recognized the name immediately."

Cami's eyes widened. She felt Connor shift in the seat next to her, as if encouraged all over again by what might be the start of a confession. The fact he'd mentioned Adriana by name, when neither she nor Connor had referred to it, was a sign he was telling the truth and he really did know this woman.

"How did you know her?" he asked.

"Not that well. We'd messaged a while ago. We'd connected online, on social media, I think. I was in town, and I drove past her place. I was thinking of going in and meeting up. But it didn't look like she was home, and then my client phoned wanting changes to the proposal. So, I didn't go in. I never saw her at all. But yes, I was there, outside her place, deliberately. Wondering if I should call her. I know you guys will twist this all the way out of context. You'll say I came here to kill her, and I didn't. It wasn't like that. And I'm not saying another thing. You wanted a confession? You got one, and it's all there is."

"Do you know Liz Hughes? Kate Warner?" Connor asked.

"I don't know them."

"Do you play Bordercross?" Cami asked.

"No. I don't. You'll find no evidence of it on my machine. I imagine that must be important to you? Maybe it should clue you in that you're on the wrong track because the only games I have time for are the ones I work on professionally. I've never played Bordercross. Never worked on it, either."

There was silence in the room for a while.

"Take a moment. We'll be back," Connor said.

They stood up and left.

Connor looked tired, Cami realized. It was getting toward evening. It felt like they'd spent hours in there with this man, talking in circles and getting nothing definite, apart from that he'd wanted to meet up with one of the victims.

But as Cami thought about the situation, she suddenly wondered if there was something else she could try in the meantime. Something else she could do.

It wouldn't hurt to try it. It would take only a few minutes to set up. And it could run, innocently, while she was back in the interrogation room questioning Leeming.

If he was guilty, then it was just a question of time.

But if he was not guilty and he was just a man with no people skills and a bad attitude, then Cami wanted to try an alternative plan.

Something Leeming himself had said had made her think of it. He'd mentioned the game, and that it was clearly an important part of the whole investigation. He'd said he hadn't played it and she had believed him. He might be lying, but she didn't think so. He seemed too smart for such a lie.

With that in mind, Cami had come up with another idea. A bold, reckless idea that might very well fail, but might just possibly get them further. Because without a doubt, the killer was in the game. Those taunting avatar visuals had confirmed it.

She wanted to access the game, create a character, and see if she could attract the killer's eye, and set herself up as his prey.

CHAPTER TWENTY SIX

Now that Cami had the idea of going into Bordercross in her head, she couldn't shift it. Surely there would be a chance that she could create a character that would lure this killer in—assuming he was not the man sitting in the interview room.

Leeming might not be the killer, but he was clearly resisting questioning every step of the way for different reasons, and it would take time to get past all the levels of resistance he was putting up. Maybe he was telling the honest truth and really had just messaged Adriana wanting to meet up. And he could have driven past Liz's house accidentally. It was in a busy area. There was a restaurant at the end of her street, and a few office parks in the neighborhood.

It would be a good idea to try another tactic at the same time. There was no way of knowing whether it would work in this situation, but she at least wanted to try.

Gaining enthusiasm for her idea, Cami knew she needed to create a character that a killer would want to meet up with, someone who would get his attention, and who would make him want to take the next step. It made sense.

"Right," Connor told her, as they trudged into the office. "We're going to take an hour's break. Leave him to cool off. See if we get a different story when we go back in."

"Connor, I've had an idea," Cami said.

Connor stared at her, with a look in his eyes that said at this point in time, and after this day, he was not ready for any idea that was a wild theory. Which hers was, of course. Cami knew she'd have to sell it to him, hard.

"What if Leeming is not the killer?" she asked.

He sighed. "That's the worst-case scenario for sure. If we can't prove anything, we'll have to start again. I'm working on his whereabouts. The Hyatt will have cameras and we can potentially try to trace his comings and goings, from the hotel at least, through the cameras. But the footage from that might only be available tomorrow unless we drive there and look through it all now."

Cami nodded. That was going to be a long process. Just as long and tortuous as finding the number plate similarities.

She checked her program again. It had finished running now but had not picked up another match in the vehicles.

But that might just mean this killer was very local, Cami decided. He might have driven to Adriana but walked to Liz. He might have taken a cab to one and a different cab to the other. If he was local, he knew the terrain, he knew his stamping ground.

Or rather his hunting ground.

"I was wondering if I should go into the game and see if I can lure him," Cami said.

"How would you do that?"

"Log in to the game. Use an IP address that doesn't connect back to a police station, maybe just link to the cell network near here, and see if I could somehow get see him and get him to follow me?"

"Would that even be possible?"

Cami shrugged. "I don't know, but he's clearly got a set of parameters in place that he's using, and one of them must be to find local people. If he has got a way of hunting for me that bypasses the network and brings up my personal information, then all he'll see is that I'm a student. He won't see that I'm law enforcement. So, he might go for it, and decide to follow me."

Connor frowned. "It's worth a try, then, but we need to go back in after an hour. So, whatever you do, make it quick, and don't get too caught up in it."

"I won't, I will make sure to be ready in an hour," Cami promised.

She felt like she was taking part in the investigation in a whole new way now.

This was where she made her mark. This was where she could have a role in catching the killer.

She felt surprisingly nervous, knowing that her theory would only work if he was online and hunting at the time.

But he might be. If he wasn't sitting in the police interview room, of course, he would be online. Surely it would take tons of research to narrow down the right victim. That research would be time consuming. Perhaps it was all part of the fun for him.

Cami logged into the game on her phone and set about creating a character that she thought would appeal to him. She remembered how the avatars had looked that he'd chosen: bright, eye-catching, and feminine.

It had to be something that would get attention. She needed to stand out, for him to stop and look at her and think, “That one’s different.” She had to sell herself to him.

Cami decided she had to be feminine too. She’d be a brunette. She’d be petite. She’d have a low neckline showing off her shapely form, with a flirty, colorful dress and high heels.

She’d have a glossy smile and big eyes.

She would create a character that was confident. The other avatars had all seemed confident. Perhaps there was something about that which this killer was drawn to. She’d be confident in her looks, but not conceited. She’d be confident in her attire and expression, but not showy.

She hoped the killer would be online when she made contact and that he would be able to see her.

She took a deep breath. She had to get this right. Once she was in the game, she couldn’t change anything.

Quickly, Cami put the finishing touches to her character. She thought it looked real. She had a low neckline and a sexy smile, she was petite and clearly feminine, she was confident, and she had a big bust, and she was wearing colorful clothing that would stand out.

Her name. She needed a good name.

Cami decided on “PaganPrincess”. A name that had appeal to it and a note of adventure.

PaganPrincess was ready to access the game.

As she entered the game world, it seemed to open up to her. She’d never appreciated the scenery and the detail that went into creating the game before. There were customized building fronts, a variety of different environments, and it was all so colorful and vivid. Her character wasn’t, though. It was fainter than the others. It hadn’t been upgraded yet. The game had notified her that her character would only be fully functional once she’d confirmed her details via email.

Cami decided to start by walking down one of the main streets. If he was around, then hopefully he’d notice her, and she’d catch his eye. And then she could be on the lookout for those who followed her, the people in common.

She hoped her reasoning was correct, and she hoped that the killer would be online and watching.

She made her way into the game. She walked confidently up the street, her heels making a clacking sound on the pavement, her eyes scanning the crowd.

Would he be watching?

And if he was, would she be able to pick it up?

Hoping that the answer to both questions was yes, she walked on, deeper into the game world, hoping that she could upgrade her character as soon as possible to get the most out of her experience here.

CHAPTER TWENTY SEVEN

Styx was hunting, in the territory he knew so well, deep in the cityscape of Bordercross. He was prowling, choosing his victims, and sending out his lures. He had code embedded deep in the system, hidden away, that allowed him to do what he did. An almost invisible and undetectable program which gave him the access he needed.

The draw of the game was addictive in itself. The thrill of the hunt, the knowledge that others were playing too. But Styx took it to a whole new level. He was addicted to what he did now. He knew it, and he didn't care.

He was sure he could continue to do this for a long while now. Sure that he would not be found out.

He walked along the virtual streets that were so familiar to him. His territory, his world. He felt at home here. He knew how the city worked, knew its rhythms. And, of course, he could spot anyone new logging in.

Styx knew it was essential to get the information he needed as soon as possible. There was no time to waste in identifying his new suspects.

Staring into the colorful images of the street ahead, he identified a few new players signing in. And then, the responses he was waiting for, as they accepted the lures. Of course they did. All new players did—well, almost all.

His fingers tapped the keyboard, opening lures, the way he had done a thousand times before. His lures were embedded deep in the game code, and they were hard to find. Impossible, actually. Only he knew, and they worked perfectly.

He glanced at his program, monitoring the response. There were some suitable candidates, and that was good, because he wanted to feel that rush, he wanted the adrenaline to pump through his system.

He wanted the kill.

He took a look at the players who had responded. Here was an interesting one that caught his eye immediately. PaganPrincess. She was a colorful character.

He watched her move, he watched her walk, he watched the way she dressed. She had some very interesting visual traits about her.

She had a low-cut top but with a flirty, cute expression. She was wearing trendy clothing that stood out. He liked the look of her. She was the kind of woman he had hopes for. As he watched, her character brightened, and he felt a surge of satisfaction. She'd upgraded!

He could imagine her sitting in her office or her study, learning about this game, applying the knowledge she already had. Probably, she was an experienced player in other games. The way she moved and interacted showed him that.

He watched her for a little longer, then decided to follow her. She was an intriguing character. She was clearly out to make an impression.

Styx followed PaganPrincess through the streets of Bordercross, while comparing the avatar with the new information he had acquired on her.

He was glad she'd upgraded, very glad. Because it told him she was a Boston local. It was almost as if he'd sensed it.

She was really quite interesting, and he found himself wondering what she was doing, what she was thinking. What made her tick? What was her story?

He was still puzzling over her when she stopped at a café. He stopped, too, watching her from outside the window.

Staring at the image of PaganPrincess, he was almost overwhelmed with the urge to kill her. To meet her in the flesh, to creep up on her while she was engrossed in her digital, artificial world. To hear the gasp of horror as she realized he was there, no longer online but in reality, in her own environment.

It gave him such a primal joy to stalk these women.

He knew their worlds and their characters. He knew, at first, that the women had no idea that he knew them, that he was in their lives, and that he was in the shadows, watching and waiting.

He was good at moving unseen, at moving unseen in the real world, and this was an essential skill for his particular brand of hunting.

He scanned at PaganPrincess's information to see what she looked like and what she had said about herself. It made him smile. A student. Looking into the information he now had about her, he saw she was a student at MIT.

But now he began to frown. An IT student? Perhaps he should be careful of those. In fact, maybe he should do more homework on her first. Especially since, in real life, she had that trendy, asymmetrical, dark hairstyle. And that reminded him of what he'd glimpsed from the camera he'd used outside his canary's house.

It had only been a glimpse, but he wanted to think it over carefully and decide on the best course of action. While he did, he glanced at the program, checking if there was someone else who had responded to his lures. He was surprised to see that there was a new one.

This one, Spylove80, was blond, tall, and mysterious looking—in Bordercross, at least. He liked the name. It sparked his imagination. She looked new and was feeling her way around. That meant she had a lot to learn about the game, and that meant that she would have an extended period of play. That was what he needed. He wanted someone who became hooked, and who spent many hours in Bordercross. That gave him the chance to do what he had to do.

When he watched her online, Styx knew that he needed to get close to her.

He gazed at Spylove80's information, while comparing it with her avatar. He smiled. He liked her.

He liked her a lot.

He watched Spylove80 for a little while longer, then he decided to follow her.

Spylove80 was a safe bet. She was the kind of player that he would enjoy.

Spylove80 walked through the streets, and then she crossed over the bridge leading to the marketplace.

He watched her for a while, and was intrigued with the way she moved, almost furtively, and yet with an air of confidence. She had a role to play, and she was playing that role.

She was a strange mix. She walked alone, but there was no sense of loneliness or fear. He could see that she was concentrating, that there was a definite purpose to her wandering.

It was clear she was becoming enchanted by the game, the same way he was.

The game had been his guide, his savior. It had given him so much. A career, a successful start. He had taken so much, but there was still more to be gained. The players. The players were his prey.

He watched Spylove80 walk around, she was obviously looking for something, she was exploring her new environment, looking at the shops and the stalls.

He followed her, moving closer as he watched her interact with other players. She was sociable, and within a short time she was involved in some kind of quest with a character called Tracker2.

Tracker2 was a dark, saturnine character, and Spylove80 was a bright, happy blonde.

The two were working together. Tracker2 was giving Spylove80 some kind of reward for something, for doing the right thing. Styx watched the way Spylove80 accepted the reward, then he watched her move on.

Styx smiled. That was all part of the game. That was exactly how it should be.

He couldn't wait to start hunting her. But now that he'd analyzed all the evidence, all the hints in his sharp, super-intelligent mind, Styx decided that it would not be wise to go out on the hunt just yet.

If things worked out the way he planned, he needed to wait closer to home.

Just in case there was going to be the chance to take a new victim, from his very doorstep. He was ready for this. He'd always known this day would arrive, and it would simply signal a shift into a new, real-life identity. He had one planned and it would be seamless.

This was going to be a new adventure, filled with risk and the prospect of his most exciting kill yet.

Logging off, Styx got up and quickly left the room.

CHAPTER TWENTY EIGHT

Cami had been playing the game for only a minute when her email pinged. It was an email from Bordercross asking for some details to reinforce the game's security. When she did, her character would receive an upgrade and be fully functional.

"In-Game Security Checklist" it was entitled. "Dear User, welcome to Bordercross. Please confirm your details to gain full access to the game."

Listed below were the details Cami had given to log in to the game. Her date of birth, her name, her area, and the email address she had used. There were a couple more details that were optional, but if she filled them in, she'd receive a hundred experience points, so who would say no?

She was about to click reply when she checked the return email address.

It all looked above board and standard, a simple request for confirmation that was not surprising—but was it? Could there somehow be more to this? she wondered. Was this a way that he was getting information on the victims, and had they been wrong about the IP addresses?

Cami's mind raced as she examined the email more carefully. There were ways of analyzing this. She had a program that could get into the email and find out more about it, tracking back to the page's source code.

Just as a precaution, Cami ran the program. It was from the gaming company, without a doubt. The return email address was entirely legitimate.

But there was something here that her program was picking up—a command within the email itself. A command to send on, to a different email address.

Cami narrowed her eyes.

The game email was normal. But the automatic forwarding address was not. It was something that had been added. Almost like a secret program running over a program, Cami realized.

Someone had set up the instruction to be forwarded. And that someone could only be the killer.

"He's someone who worked on the game in the past," Cami realized.

She let out a long breath as finally, she realized how this had been done. It was a software engineer. Not Rowan, the game owner. But perhaps one of his employees, someone that he'd used in the past. One of the hundreds of people his lawyers had referred to, and perhaps one who'd left on bad terms.

Someone, somewhere, had gotten into this game and had set up this almost invisible and undetectable instruction. There was no way of tracing it, but now she knew more about who this person was. This was how he was able to narrow down his victims. Because, by receiving a copy of the return email, he would know their date of birth, their email address, their name, and the area where they lived. He would also know their IP address.

It was all innocent enough information, but it could be used to find them. From being anonymous people in a game, they had now become living, breathing targets that could be located and were vulnerable.

She sat up, her heart racing. Her mouth was dry. She had to get out of there, now.

She looked at the instructions on the screen. They were innocent enough. She could click reply and confirm them. She could continue playing the game.

In fact, she had to. Because without them, there was no way the killer might be prompted to target her.

She had only to click reply, confirm the details, and then she could carry on with the game.

She wondered if the killer was watching online even now. Was he waiting for her to be lured, to be trapped? If he was online, where was he? Was he watching her?

She had no choice. She clicked Reply, and watched the email disappear with a sick feeling in her stomach that her information was going elsewhere. That didn't sit well with her at all.

But it meant she now, finally, knew how the killer was working.

There was a way to find who he was and track him down. He was a software developer who, at some stage, had worked on Bordercross.

She realized, too, that he must have had access to the game's programming. That was how he had been able to put those instructions in there in the first place.

It was a worrying thought. There were so many people involved in what was essentially the creation of a massive game. It was hard to know who could be involved in such a way.

He had, somewhere, in the past, left an instruction to all new users.

She could track that information.

It must be someone who had left on bad terms, that was Cami's suspicion. Perhaps he'd started doing this as a form of payback and his methods had escalated.

It all made sense to her now.

"Connor!" she called.

"You got something?" he asked.

"Yes! Have the lawyers sent anything through?"

"Rowan's lawyers?"

"Yes."

"Yes. That list just hit my computer."

"I think there's a very strong chance one of the people on that list had something to do with this."

"Why do you say that?" he asked curiously.

"Because I've found something. Something overwritten in the email reply. It sends the response on to a forwarding address. And this could only have been put in place by someone coding."

"So, someone working on the game?"

"Yes. It must have been done very carefully, added into the code so that nobody noticed. Then the person left, but the code stayed, hidden away. Forwarding the generated responses. It's been very, very cleverly done. And without a doubt, this person is an IT expert."

"And where does it forward them to?" Connor asked.

"I don't know," Cami said.

"So, all we have is the list of names?"

"Yes, that's all we have."

Connor nodded thoughtfully. "That's brilliant of you to figure it out. Who would have thought that Rowan himself would have provided the information we need? So, let's go over what we do know about this man, because we're going to have to identify him from the list."

"He definitely lives in Boston, and that might not be common," Cami said. "The IT specialists could come from all over. But I feel he's local. He's been looking for local people so far."

"Yes. I think that has to be correct. He's started hunting in his home territory."

Connor was busy calling up the list on his computer. Cami waited impatiently. That list would be all-important.

"We're looking for someone who is most likely angry, determined, and arrogant. But all the same, a very good and talented programmer."

"Yes. It's a good theory," Connor agreed.

"And we have to work fast," Cami said. "We don't know if he's online at the moment. I think he probably is."

She glanced again at the game.

She'd noticed a few characters that she suspected might be this killer. She guessed he would be unobtrusive. He would choose an identity that would allow him to blend into the background. That was what she had decided was most likely.

But there might be a trace of him, based on that strange email instruction he'd given, that must be embedded into the game's software, and perhaps there was a way of linking it to his character.

Cami's fingers flew as she adjusted her program and widened its net.

It wasn't going to be a hundred percent reliable. Not with the quick fix she'd used. But if it gave her ninety percent, that was a start, wasn't it?

She tapped her fingers on the desk as the program ran, scanning the characters in her visual field. One by one, they were cleared.

Apart from one.

As it reached this character, the program paused and seemed to hang. Cami knew it must be following the path of logic she'd set for it and going deeper. And that surely pointed to anomalies in the code. She leaned forward, excited, as she waited for the result.

But as she did, an error message began flashing up.

The character had gone. He'd abruptly vanished from the screen while her program was analyzing him.

But she remembered who she was. She knew his avatar, she had it in her mind. Styx was his name. And Styx was gone.

That could only mean one thing. That Styx had identified a victim in the game and was now on the hunt for her in real life.

CHAPTER TWENTY NINE

"Styx. That's his name. For now, at least. He probably has others," Cami muttered. She felt adrenaline surging through her. She had no idea whether Styx was going to try to track her or was going to pursue a different target. She was in the game, but so were a few others who seemed like they would fit his specifications.

And this was how he knew who people were. He'd been blind copied on the confirmation emails that had to be sent before people were allowed to fully participate in the game. Emails that gave a return email address, a city of residence, a date of birth, and a few other details. Enough, for sure, to track a person in real life most of the time.

And now, Styx was gone. He'd left the game and was pursuing his latest victim, but she didn't know whether he was doing that online at home, finding out her details, or whether he was already out on the streets of Boston.

Cami felt breathless at the thought that this killer was still anonymous, and there was no way of predicting who he would be targeting. Their only solution, the only way of finding him, would be to look at Rowan's list and see if they could find Styx himself.

"Styx," she said. She could do more online, but now, as things stood, it would be too time consuming. This was the moment for Connor's analytical skills and strengths to come into play.

"We'll find him," Connor told her. "And we'll catch him. We'll get him."

He got on the phone. "Ethan!" he barked. "We've got an urgent situation here. The suspect is identified. He's an ex-employee of Virtual Ventures. He used to work on Bordercross. He left code in the game that forwards player details to him."

"So, he'd be on the list we've just received from Rowan's lawyers?" Ethan said.

"He will. We need you to collaborate with our BAU agents. I'm going to set up a teleconference. We have literally over a hundred names here. Now the killer is among them. So, let's go through what we know."

“He’s a Boston resident,” Cami said. “And from the evidence, most likely a male.”

“Boston resident. He’s local. He’s chosen his targets here,” Connor agreed.

“He may have left on bad terms.”

“Look for a dismissal, a firing or a sudden resignation,” Connor advised his team. “It’s more likely he’ll have done that.”

Cami felt her blood surge. This was like a race. A race where life and death were vying for the finish line. It was all too possible he might be out, looking to kill again.

“He’s capable of violence. But that doesn’t mean he might have a record. He’s highly intelligent, and his violent tendencies might end up being suppressed, or channeled into something that seems normal.”

“We’re looking. We’re checking the list. We’ve got the profiles and addresses being loaded now,” Ethan said.

“We’ll work from the bottom on our side,” Connor said. Quickly, he directed Cami. “Take the names. Input them into this database. You’ll get address details and a phone number. Hopefully, all current. Then cross-check with what the list says. We’re then going to rank the suspects in order of their strength and probability.”

“On it,” Cami said.

As fast as she could, Cami did her work, inputting the names and details of the list. She could hear the FBI researchers and BAU agents doing the same, wearing headphones, talking to each other over their phones, and she heard them cross-checking the names she was providing.

She felt herself racing, racing to get the information out and to get her work done.

“We’re looking at the Social Security details,” Ethan confirmed. “Most of these are current. And we’re cross-referencing the names with the ones you’ve already input from the list. The ones that are a match are the top of the list. The ones that aren’t are becoming less likely to be the suspects as we go down.”

Cami’s hands were flying over the keyboard.

She was ranking the names on their likelihood. The computer was doing the same, and the phone was ringing. Ethan and Connor were talking on the phone, and Cami heard Connor say, “We can’t be sure,” and Ethan reply, “It’s pretty much sure.” She closed out their conversation and focused on her own job.

"The profile is narrowing," Connor said to her. "We're getting a top ten. But that's not enough. We need a top two. A top three. We can't send ten teams out. We need to make sure we rush to the most likely ones first. Work on it further."

Who was he?

Now that all the information had been assessed, the computer was flashing up the names who appeared to match the profile most closely.

"Those should be the most likely."

Eagerly, Cami looked forward, reading the list of employees that had now been ranked according to their likelihood of being the suspect.

There were three of them.

The first was Aaron Rose. The second was Lucius Donovan, and the third was Roger Stokes.

Quickly, feeling breathless, Cami read the details on the three suspects.

Aaron Rose, age twenty-eight, had worked for Bordercross two years ago. He'd been fired and had gone on to work for a competitor. He lived in suburban Boston and from the file, he seemed to be married with two kids.

Lucius Donovan, age thirty, had quit his job six months ago, walking out one day. He was single and lived alone, and his address was in downtown Boston.

Roger Stokes, age twenty-six, had worked for Bordercross until three months ago, when he was fired. He currently owned a house on the outskirts of town, and he was single.

Cami felt her heart thumping. She looked at the screen. This could be it. One of these names was who it could be.

"We're checking the physical addresses," Ethan confirmed.

"We need to get agents to each of the addresses," Connor said, his voice clipped and alert. "And be prepared. This guy is capable of violence. Be prepared for anything."

"Who do you and Cami want to take?" Ethan asked Connor.

Cami sat straighter. They were going out too? She'd expected it, but yet she hadn't.

Chasing down a dangerous, violent criminal, a killer. She knew she had to go. She would be there. She would help, although she wasn't sure how. But there was no way she was going to back out of this.

As soon as she'd seen the names, Cami had grabbed her phone, looking for any information on these three, anything that could possibly narrow the parameters further.

They all listed gaming as their hobby as well as their work on social media, she saw.

And researching further, she saw that Aaron was on a group that engaged in very dark and violent chat. Would that make it more likely or less likely? She didn't know but was going to say less likely. The group could be an outlet. The killer would have his sadistic urges pent-up, not expressed to anyone but himself.

"Aaron might be my third choice," she said nervously.

She thought that Roger Stokes was her first choice but that was just based on his physical appearance. He looked more aggressive than the others, but she couldn't exactly say that.

"Let's choose the other two first, then. Ethan, you take Roger Stokes. We'll take Lucius Donovan. We'll talk again once they're ruled out and move on to the next on the list."

Connor stood up and stared at Cami, and now she saw Connor in his element, a man of action, an experienced agent. Suddenly, she saw him more clearly, and understood better why he acted the way he did. Why he was sometimes so stern and came across as so controlling.

He sounded calm and resolute as he told her, "Come on. We're going to go catch this killer."

CHAPTER THIRTY

As Cami rushed out of the office, she felt extremely nervous. She was scared for the two of them, and she was scared for Ethan and his partner, too, as well as for the other team, racing to the third of the three most likely criminals.

If the profiling was right, then one of them might be coming up against a dangerous and violent killer in a very short time. That was a terrifying thought.

She pulled up Lucius's picture, looking at it carefully. He was a preppy looking guy, with blue eyes, brown hair, and regular features. Not the type of guy you'd think would be a killer.

She didn't know what to expect. She was in territory she knew nothing about, but she felt eager to go with Connor and do what she could.

They jumped into his car and Connor pulled off, racing toward downtown with the siren on.

"What happens if he's not home?" she asked.

"We'll track his cellphone number. We'll do what we need to. But we must start by going to his residence."

He might still be home, doing research, or he might be out, ready to make a kill. Which would it be? Cami wondered. The short drive felt like it took an eternity. She was filled with tension and expectation.

Here was his street. In the early evening, the road was busy with traffic coming and going. It was a lively part of town. Connor raced down the road, and they stopped outside the small, well equipped looking home where he lived.

Cami stared at it, feeling excited that they'd finally arrived. The house looked so normal. A pretty, single-story home built in a modern style, with curtains closed and blinds down. Light shimmered from beyond, indicating someone might be at home.

They climbed out of the car, and Connor turned to her.

"Stay back. I'm going to take a walk around the house here and do a recce before we go any further. I want to know what the exit points are, and whether he looks to be home. If we knock on the front, I don't want him getting out the back. I'll be a minute, but I need you to stay by the car. I don't want you walking into danger."

"Understood."

He handed her his phone.

"And hold this, please. If Ethan calls, if he's found the killer, then come and get me immediately, and we'll go there." He paused. "If there's any sign of danger, if this man comes out, then get in the car, lock the door, and lean on the horn."

"I'll do that."

Cami was aware how even this short, routine check was fraught with danger.

She waited by the car, holding Connor's phone, watching the house intently.

Would Connor flush him out? Was he even at home? There were a couple of lights on inside, but not many. But then, an IT expert wouldn't need many when they were at work. A glowing screen would be all they required, and one or two lamps, perhaps. She knew what techies were like—after all, she was one of them herself. When coding, they were immersed in their own world.

What would she do if she were him? she wondered. She thought she would have thought ahead. She would be watching out for police. She was worried Connor was going into serious danger. Would he hide, or would he be looking to ambush?

She heard the purring noise of a car on the road behind her, but barely looked around as she watched Connor move from window to window, before disappearing around the side of the house.

There was a click.

What was it? Her senses were focused on what was ahead of her, not what was behind.

But too late, the hairs on the back of her neck prickled as she heard a soft sound behind her. In shock, she began to turn.

She realized, too late, that the sound she'd heard had been a car door opening. The car had stopped, and someone had gotten out.

As she started to turn, someone grabbed her from behind, grasping the collar of her jacket, yanking her back, the grip so tight and sudden that she shrieked aloud. Immediately, a strong hand clamped over her mouth, stifling the sound.

"So, it's you. You in the baseball cap?" a voice hissed in her ear.

Connor's phone was wrenched from her hand. He had it, and a moment later he flung it to the ground. Cami heard a shattering noise as he stamped on it, and then the grip on her collar was back, tighter this time, and she was being dragged backward.

"I've been watching you. Waiting for you. I knew you'd come here. And now, we're going to get rid of you."

Cami struggled furiously, but the man was too quick. Too strong. He yanked her hand up behind her, so she screamed in pain, the sound muffled by his palm. And then he shoved her toward the car's open trunk.

It was a spacious, white car. The trunk looked dark. No way could she go in there, Cami thought, no way. This couldn't be happening! He was abducting her. In an instant, she'd landed in danger.

He yanked her hand up again so that the pain paralyzed her and the next moment, he was shoving her forward so that she sprawled into the carpeted cubicle.

She kicked out furiously, but he was ready for her. He grabbed her legs and shoved them in, and then as she writhed around, getting ready to face him, desperately trying to get out, the lid slammed.

She was left in the utter darkness, disoriented and scared.

The next moment, with a jolt, the car started up and they were driving away at full speed.

"No!" Cami screamed, hoping someone would hear, but the thick carpet in the trunk swallowed her voice. The ride was a veering, disorienting rollercoaster journey as the car accelerated and swung.

He hadn't been out waiting for a victim, Cami realized. He'd been out waiting for her. That was why he'd signed off on the game. To prepare. He'd known that they were hunting. He must have recognized her from that brief glimpse he'd had from the camera. He was cleverer and more paranoid than she'd dreamed.

What could she do now? She kicked at the lid, but it was thick and solid, and in the small space, she couldn't get leverage. There was no way she could break out of here; she wasn't strong enough. And when he opened the lid, when this hell ride was over, Cami knew it would be too late. She'd be facing death.

For a minute, having lost control of the situation, she was so scared that she couldn't think straight, and for Cami, whose logical thought was the underpinnings of her whole identity, this felt more terrifying than anything.

But she was not going to let herself be too scared to act. Not for long. Perhaps she was going to die. But she was not going to give up. No way. She had to get out now. It was now or never.

He'd grabbed the phone from her hand.

As her whirling thoughts slowly subsided enough for her to reason her way through the situation, Cami realized that he'd grabbed a phone. He'd grabbed what she'd been holding—looking to disarm her of her weapon, which he knew she could use.

But he hadn't grabbed her phone. She'd been holding Connor's phone. She still had hers with her in the inside pocket of her FBI jacket, which he hadn't checked.

He'd made a mistake and given her an opportunity.

She couldn't call Connor because his phone was now broken. But she could call somebody. She could call Ethan. She could use what she had.

Cami fumbled for her phone, dragging it from her jacket. In the darkness and on this wild ride, it was difficult to get it out. She had to wedge herself in the trunk to keep herself still, bracing her head against the carpet, her feet against the opposite side, her breathing coming fast and rapid, because she had no idea how much time she had or how soon this would be over.

She dialed Ethan's number.

He answered immediately. "Cami? We've got no sign of our suspect this side. What's up your side?"

"I've been taken," she said breathlessly. "He got me while Connor was checking his house."

"What? Where are you?" His voice was urgent.

Cami did her best to work at speed to give him the salient facts.

"I'm in the trunk of a car. I don't know what type it is. White. And an electric car," she gabbled. "He took Connor's phone. I was holding it. He smashed it."

"We're on it. We'll get to you. We'll track your phone," Ethan said, but she could hear the undertone of tension in his voice. "I'll get hold of Connor on the radio. We're coming to you now, Cami. Just hang in there."

"I'll activate my live location," she said, hoping signal would hold.

With shaking hands, Cami activated her live location.

"Cami, I'm not seeing it." Ethan sounded desperate.

"Perhaps it's taking time. Perhaps you'll start to see it."

She had no idea why it wasn't working. Perhaps there was a delay in the interface. Perhaps the GPS signal in the area where she was was bad. There could be tall buildings briefly blocking it and making it more difficult to track.

"I'm going to Connor. I'll call you when I get to him if I don't find the signal," Ethan said. He cut the call.

She knew she'd just have to hope that Ethan would pick up the signal, but this delay filled her with fear.

She had no idea how far away Ethan was, or how quickly he'd be able to get ahold of Connor. Connor could have left the car and gone looking for her, thinking she'd gone somewhere on some mission with his phone.

This would all take time. She didn't know how much of it she had.

What else could she do, Cami thought. What else could she possibly do?

The car veered again, and she pushed against the carpeted sides to try and keep herself still. This ride was so disorienting that she was feeling sick.

But she'd had an idea. Something she could try and do, while clinging to the hope that Ethan was powering toward her, but with no idea if he'd be in time or not.

This was an electric car.

If she could access the controls, perhaps she could do something. Perhaps that would be the only thing she could do in time. She had a program that could ping nearby devices. It was on her phone, and she could hopefully access it quickly.

Knowing this would be her last attempt at getting away, Cami began to run the program.

CHAPTER THIRTY ONE

In the darkness of the car's trunk, on a swaying, battering ride that she knew would end in death, Cami did her best to suppress her panic.

She accessed the program, feeling frustrated that she was so slow, because her fingers kept being jolted off the keyboard. She fought for control, fought in the darkness.

She had the program up, but a button was flashing on the screen, because it had lost connection.

But Cami wasn't going to give up now.

She hit the button and the program did what it could. It began searching, to see if there were any nearby devices or electronics connected up.

There it was. "Tesla X." That was her prison. That was where she was trapped. What could she do? Was there any way she could at least activate its geolocation to help Ethan find her?

Or could she do more?

There would be a way into this operating system, she was sure of it. But it would take time. That was what she didn't have as time was working against her now.

Her heart was pounding.

She couldn't let panic take over. Forcing herself to be strong, she knew she had to use what she had.

Cami fought to keep a steady breathing rhythm in her dark prison, the only light coming from her screen.

Her phone's battery was low. She saw that with another surge of concern. Everything she was doing was draining the device. She was in the car, in the dark, and there was no way to charge her phone. She hadn't had a chance to charge it earlier as she was so busy hunting for the killer.

Little did she knew he'd been hunting for her too.

She didn't have much time, Cami knew.

There wasn't enough time to get into this car's operating system. But what else was here? There was something else in this car that her program was picking up.

The car veered around a corner and Cami heard brakes screech. She flinched, banging her head against the lid, feeling her hands icy cold with adrenaline.

It was a satellite tracking and maintenance system. The car had a remote tracker installed.

Now that would be easier to get into. Cami's mind flew, her fingers were less fast, but this would require fewer steps to take over. If she could trick this device into believing the vehicle had been reported stolen, then she could take it over. She could take over the controls.

With the cramped space feeling hot and airless, dizzy from the ride and the stress, Cami worked furiously.

There. She was in.

She pressed the key to disable the car, to turn the engine off, hoping it would work, praying this would get her somewhere.

It didn't work.

All she got was a red, flashing Error message.

Why? Why was she getting this?

Cami's heart hammered furiously. Why, at this critical time, with her phone almost ready to die, could she not access the system to stop the car? She was in! Why this error?

Cami was hyperventilating with stress. Really? At this time, technology was refusing to cooperate? And then, she realized.

The button would only work if the car was stopped. The program would not allow the car to be disabled while in motion. It was a safety feature, presumably.

She wished she could see where this car was headed on its wild, veering ride. Perhaps the only time he'd stop would be at the end. Perhaps he was already on a long stretch of road, racing to the destination he had in mind for her.

Or perhaps he was still in an urban area, with stop signs and traffic lights, and at some stage, the car would come to a stop.

But how soon?

She literally had five percent of battery left on her phone. The live tracking, that she hoped was working, was draining it. Communicating with the satellite tracking device was draining it more.

She might have only a minute left.

Which would happen first?

If the phone died, it would be a catastrophe. The live locator would stop. Ethan wouldn't find her. Cami had no doubt this would signal her death. She had to get the satellite tracker to stop the car. She willed him to stop, visualizing a traffic light, a stop sign, some reason for him to have to pause this murderous ride.

And then, she felt the car slow, felt the brakes activate.

Stop, stop, she pleaded, breathing the word as she watched her phone's screen, now in battery saving mode, dimmer than it had been.

The car slowed further. And then, it stopped.

Like lightning, Cami's finger was on the button. And she felt the engine cut. She felt the car power down. She'd done it! She'd gotten control and had brought the vehicle to a halt.

Now, could she get herself out of here?

Auto unlock. There it was. That was the command she needed.

Cami slammed her finger against the button.

The trunk flew open, daylight blinding her. She scrambled out and slammed it. She was in a practically deserted industrial area. He'd stopped outside a garage that he must have been intending to open, a garage that would have been her grave.

And, in the blinding light, she saw that he'd seen her. She saw his face, pale through the window. And she saw the door start to open.

He was coming for her. He was coming out.

"No!" Cami screamed. "No!"

She lunged for the door and threw her full weight against it, wrestling it shut, hearing his angry cry and knowing that now she needed to do the final thing that could save her, in the split second she had left.

With almost no battery left, Cami pressed the system command to lock the doors again.

They snapped shut.

She breathed a sigh of relief. In emergency mode, she knew the driver could not reactivate the door opening. This car was now locked down solid, and he was inside.

Just before her phone died, she saw a message from Ethan had come through.

"Got signal! On the way!"

Cami breathed deeply. She was shaking all over. She couldn't believe she'd escaped death by such a narrow margin. She felt lightheaded from shock. Her legs felt like cotton wool.

And then, Cami heard a hammering noise coming from the front of the car.

Curious and hesitant, she peered around.

There was Lucius. With a face contorted in rage, he was hammering on the window glass, trying desperately to force his way out of the car that had become his prison.

Already, Cami could hear sirens in the distance. Her backup was arriving.

She walked over to the window and stared through the tinted glass at the face of the killer, taking in his ineffectual rage, watching him bash futilely against the window.

And then, Cami moved around, sitting on the car's bonnet, hearing him yell aloud in fury as he saw her, so close but so far, and realized how trapped he was.

Feeling calmer now, feeling as if he deserved every minute of his rage and fear and helplessness, she perched on the bonnet, watching him through the windscreen as she waited for the FBI team to arrive.

EPILOGUE

Cami breathed a sigh of relief as she walked over to her laptop. She placed a hand on its lid, feeling a rush of fondness for the state-of-the-art machine that was her most valuable possession by far.

"I've missed you," she said, staring around the tiny apartment in the university residence, feeling as happy as if she'd been reunited with a long-lost friend.

She couldn't believe what had happened in the past two days. She'd been arrested as a felon, co-opted by the FBI, and she'd chased down a killer and managed to outwit him at the last possible moment.

Connor had congratulated her afterward when they were wrapping up the case in the evening. And Fraser had too! The big boss had stopped in to tell her that she'd done well.

"That was a good result, Cami Lark," he'd praised her.

She'd had a text from Jacenta, her probation officer. Jacenta had also congratulated her and confirmed the charges against her had been dropped.

And she'd enjoyed the ride back from the scene of Lucius's arrest. With Connor still wrapping things up on site, Cami had ridden back in Ethan's car. They'd had a good conversation. She felt there was a friendship developing between them. Maybe more.

A friendship with potential. With a spark.

Ethan had said that he hoped Cami was able to help with other cases. And in the future, there might be that possibility. Connor had hinted at it too. He'd said that she could expect a call from Fraser the next time they came across a tech case that could use her skills.

Most definitely, the FBI was not all bad. There were some good, fun people there. Ethan was an interesting guy. She liked his vision and his passion for his job. His own respect for Connor was even helping her understand him better.

But in the meantime, she was glad to be back here, in this apartment that was small and cozy, filled with the familiarity of home.

And there was one more urgent job she needed to do that she'd been putting off for far too long.

That conversation in the piercing studio felt like a hundred years ago, but although Cami's life had changed, she knew that Bella's mother was still being bullied.

Finally, with her phone and laptop at her fingertips, Cami had the resources to get into this bully's phone.

Sitting on the bed, absorbed in her task, she worked fast. She let the program run and watched it, sending good vibes its way.

And it got in. She drew in an excited breath. She'd done it—partially, at any rate. Now, she did have limited access to Tony's phone. She could see his texts and chat messages.

Cami raised her eyebrows.

Oh, this was lovely. This was definitely usable.

This idiot, who'd been so vicious and unfair to Bella's mother, had been chatting nonstop on his private groups and friend networks. He'd criticized the company he worked for, criticized his bosses, and said terrible things about the management, especially the women in top management.

This was totally slanderous. The comments were clearly untrue, sexist, and derogatory, and they had been shared with quite a few people.

Well, she was about to share them with many more.

Cami took screen shots of all the comments, making sure to show the name of the bully who had written them and also to whom they had been sent.

Then she looked up the company's top management, logged into an anonymous email account, and sent off the screen shots to them.

She smiled in satisfaction as the emails went on their way. Pretty soon—like, first thing tomorrow morning, she was sure a world of trouble would be heading this man's way. Hopefully, he'd be fired on the spot and then Bella's mother would have a chance to be happy and do her work in peace.

Before she closed her laptop, another thought occurred to her, so tempting and sudden that she could not resist it.

Now that she was with the FBI, and knew the login details to get into the case files, could she look at the old, cold cases? Would she be able to access the old files from her sister Jenna's case, and see what had happened, and why the case had stalled, and what exactly had played out?

It was an idea too tempting to ignore. Before she could think too hard about it, Cami quickly logged in.

Here was the database. Here was the now-familiar screen.

And here were the warnings flashing up as she accessed the archives, warnings which she ignored.

"Privileged information. Authorized personnel only may access."

And then, the big one.

"Password needed."

Fingers flying, with guilt creeping inside her but deciding it was worth the risk just to see, that nobody would know, she tried the basic hack that usually worked quickly to solve passwords of medium strength.

There. She was in.

She took a look at the case files, which were arranged by year, stretching back in time. Cami quickly clicked on the year she needed and went hunting for the name. Jenna Lark. Was she here?

She felt breathless with tension and excitement, flushed with guilt, but unable to stop. She just wanted to see. It was not really breaking the rules, was it? Just bending them.

Here was the case! Her heart accelerated.

The FBI had handled it. So, what had happened? Why had it not been solved, what had they found?

It would be possible, Cami thought, to copy the files over. She worked at top speed, downloading and duplicating them. She didn't want to spend too long in here. She could not risk being found out.

But, as she began copying the files, Cami realized there was something strange happening.

Something very weird, that shouldn't have been able to be done at all.

While she was duplicating the file, it was erasing part of itself.

It was as if the digital record had been programmed to delete certain information if it was ever accessed.

Cami drew in a sharp breath.

There was something in this case that people didn't want her to know.

Something that nobody was supposed to know.

Somebody in the FBI had set this to run. Someone was hiding something about her sister's case. Now, she only had part of the information, and the full details might never be discovered.

The FBI was not the perfect, pristine organization they liked to believe they were. There were people in it who had things to hide and who were working against it. This was clear evidence of it, even though

Cami realized that thanks to the way she'd gotten it, it was her evidence alone as it could not be shared.

"Who are you?" Cami asked under her breath, feeling her mistrust flare up again.

And then, in a stronger voice, she added, "You can't hide. And you won't hide. Whoever you are, I'm going to find you."

NOW AVAILABLE!

JUST OUTSIDE
(A Cami Lark Mystery—Book 2)

With her tattoos and piercings, MIT tech genius Cami Lark is rebellious and anti-authoritarian—and finds herself in deep trouble when she hacks the FBI. Faced with the choice of prison or aiding the BAU hunt down serial killers, Cami reluctantly partners. But when a a spree of online killings hits close to home, Cami may find herself at a loss—and the next target.

"A masterpiece of thriller and mystery."
—Books and Movie Reviews, Roberto Mattos (re Once Gone)

JUST OUTSIDE (A Cami Lark FBI Suspense Thriller—Book 2) is the second novel in a new series by #1 bestseller and USA Today bestselling author Blake Pierce, whose bestseller Once Gone (a free download) has received over 7,000 five star ratings and reviews.

A page-turning and harrowing crime thriller featuring a brilliant and tortured FBI agent, the CAMI LARK series is a riveting mystery, packed with non-stop action, suspense, twists and turns, revelations, and driven by a breakneck pace that will keep you flipping pages late into the night. Fans of Rachel Caine, Teresa Driscoll and Robert Dugoni are sure to fall in love.

Books #3-#5 in the series—JUST RIGHT, JUST FORGET, and JUST ONCE—are also available.

"An edge of your seat thriller in a new series that keeps you turning pages! ...So many twists, turns and red herrings… I can't wait to see what happens next."
—Reader review (Her Last Wish)

"A strong, complex story about two FBI agents trying to stop a serial killer. If you want an author to capture your attention and have you guessing, yet trying to put the pieces together, Pierce is your author!"
—Reader review (Her Last Wish)

"A typical Blake Pierce twisting, turning, roller coaster ride suspense thriller. Will have you turning the pages to the last sentence of the last chapter!!!"
—Reader review (City of Prey)

"Right from the start we have an unusual protagonist that I haven't seen done in this genre before. The action is nonstop… A very atmospheric novel that will keep you turning pages well into the wee hours."
—Reader review (City of Prey)

"Everything that I look for in a book… a great plot, interesting characters, and grabs your interest right away. The book moves along at a breakneck pace and stays that way until the end. Now on go I to book two!"
—Reader review (Girl, Alone)

"Exciting, heart pounding, edge of your seat book… a must read for mystery and suspense readers!"
—Reader review (Girl, Alone)

Blake Pierce

Blake Pierce is the USA Today bestselling author of the RILEY PAGE mystery series, which includes seventeen books. Blake Pierce is also the author of the MACKENZIE WHITE mystery series, comprising fourteen books; of the AVERY BLACK mystery series, comprising six books; of the KERI LOCKE mystery series, comprising five books; of the MAKING OF RILEY PAIGE mystery series, comprising six books; of the KATE WISE mystery series, comprising seven books; of the CHLOE FINE psychological suspense mystery, comprising six books; of the JESSIE HUNT psychological suspense thriller series, comprising twenty six books; of the AU PAIR psychological suspense thriller series, comprising three books; of the ZOE PRIME mystery series, comprising six books; of the ADELE SHARP mystery series, comprising sixteen books, of the EUROPEAN VOYAGE cozy mystery series, comprising six books; of the LAURA FROST FBI suspense thriller, comprising eleven books; of the ELLA DARK FBI suspense thriller, comprising fourteen books (and counting); of the A YEAR IN EUROPE cozy mystery series, comprising nine books, of the AVA GOLD mystery series, comprising six books (and counting); of the RACHEL GIFT mystery series, comprising ten books (and counting); of the VALERIE LAW mystery series, comprising nine books (and counting); of the PAIGE KING mystery series, comprising eight books (and counting); of the MAY MOORE mystery series, comprising eleven books (and counting); the CORA SHIELDS mystery series, comprising five books (and counting); of the NICKY LYONS mystery series, comprising five books (and counting), and of the new CAMI LARK mystery series, comprising five books (and counting).

An avid reader and lifelong fan of the mystery and thriller genres, Blake loves to hear from you, so please feel free to visit www.blakepierceauthor.com to learn more and stay in touch.

BOOKS BY BLAKE PIERCE

CAMI LARK MYSTERY SERIES

JUST ME (Book #1)

JUST OUTSIDE (Book #2)

JUST RIGHT (Book #3)

JUST FORGET (Book #4)

JUST ONCE (Book #5)

NICKY LYONS MYSTERY SERIES

ALL MINE (Book #1)

ALL HIS (Book #2)

ALL HE SEES (Book #3)

ALL ALONE (Book #4)

ALL FOR ONE (Book #5)

CORA SHIELDS MYSTERY SERIES

UNDONE (Book #1)

UNWANTED (Book #2)

UNHINGED (Book #3)

UNSAID (Book #4)

UNGLUED (Book #5)

MAY MOORE SUSPENSE THRILLER

NEVER RUN (Book #1)

NEVER TELL (Book #2)

NEVER LIVE (Book #3)

NEVER HIDE (Book #4)

NEVER FORGIVE (Book #5)

NEVER AGAIN (Book #6)

NEVER LOOK BACK (Book #7)

NEVER FORGET (Book #8)

NEVER LET GO (Book #9)

NEVER PRETEND (Book #10)

NEVER HESITATE (Book #11)

PAIGE KING MYSTERY SERIES

THE GIRL HE PINED (Book #1)
THE GIRL HE CHOSE (Book #2)
THE GIRL HE TOOK (Book #3)
THE GIRL HE WISHED (Book #4)
THE GIRL HE CROWNED (Book #5)
THE GIRL HE WATCHED (Book #6)
THE GIRL HE WANTED (Book #7)
THE GIRL HE CLAIMED (Book #8)

VALERIE LAW MYSTERY SERIES
NO MERCY (Book #1)
NO PITY (Book #2)
NO FEAR (Book #3)
NO SLEEP (Book #4)
NO QUARTER (Book #5)
NO CHANCE (Book #6)
NO REFUGE (Book #7)
NO GRACE (Book #8)
NO ESCAPE (Book #9)

RACHEL GIFT MYSTERY SERIES
HER LAST WISH (Book #1)
HER LAST CHANCE (Book #2)
HER LAST HOPE (Book #3)
HER LAST FEAR (Book #4)
HER LAST CHOICE (Book #5)
HER LAST BREATH (Book #6)
HER LAST MISTAKE (Book #7)
HER LAST DESIRE (Book #8)
HER LAST REGRET (Book #9)
HER LAST HOUR (Book #10)

AVA GOLD MYSTERY SERIES
CITY OF PREY (Book #1)
CITY OF FEAR (Book #2)
CITY OF BONES (Book #3)
CITY OF GHOSTS (Book #4)
CITY OF DEATH (Book #5)
CITY OF VICE (Book #6)

A YEAR IN EUROPE
A MURDER IN PARIS (Book #1)
DEATH IN FLORENCE (Book #2)
VENGEANCE IN VIENNA (Book #3)
A FATALITY IN SPAIN (Book #4)

ELLA DARK FBI SUSPENSE THRILLER
GIRL, ALONE (Book #1)
GIRL, TAKEN (Book #2)
GIRL, HUNTED (Book #3)
GIRL, SILENCED (Book #4)
GIRL, VANISHED (Book 5)
GIRL ERASED (Book #6)
GIRL, FORSAKEN (Book #7)
GIRL, TRAPPED (Book #8)
GIRL, EXPENDABLE (Book #9)
GIRL, ESCAPED (Book #10)
GIRL, HIS (Book #11)
GIRL, LURED (Book #12)
GIRL, MISSING (Book #13)
GIRL, UNKNOWN (Book #14)

LAURA FROST FBI SUSPENSE THRILLER
ALREADY GONE (Book #1)
ALREADY SEEN (Book #2)
ALREADY TRAPPED (Book #3)
ALREADY MISSING (Book #4)
ALREADY DEAD (Book #5)
ALREADY TAKEN (Book #6)
ALREADY CHOSEN (Book #7)
ALREADY LOST (Book #8)
ALREADY HIS (Book #9)
ALREADY LURED (Book #10)
ALREADY COLD (Book #11)

EUROPEAN VOYAGE COZY MYSTERY SERIES
MURDER (AND BAKLAVA) (Book #1)
DEATH (AND APPLE STRUDEL) (Book #2)
CRIME (AND LAGER) (Book #3)
MISFORTUNE (AND GOUDA) (Book #4)

CALAMITY (AND A DANISH) (Book #5)
MAYHEM (AND HERRING) (Book #6)

ADELE SHARP MYSTERY SERIES
LEFT TO DIE (Book #1)
LEFT TO RUN (Book #2)
LEFT TO HIDE (Book #3)
LEFT TO KILL (Book #4)
LEFT TO MURDER (Book #5)
LEFT TO ENVY (Book #6)
LEFT TO LAPSE (Book #7)
LEFT TO VANISH (Book #8)
LEFT TO HUNT (Book #9)
LEFT TO FEAR (Book #10)
LEFT TO PREY (Book #11)
LEFT TO LURE (Book #12)
LEFT TO CRAVE (Book #13)
LEFT TO LOATHE (Book #14)
LEFT TO HARM (Book #15)
LEFT TO RUIN (Book #16)

THE AU PAIR SERIES
ALMOST GONE (Book#1)
ALMOST LOST (Book #2)
ALMOST DEAD (Book #3)

ZOE PRIME MYSTERY SERIES
FACE OF DEATH (Book#1)
FACE OF MURDER (Book #2)
FACE OF FEAR (Book #3)
FACE OF MADNESS (Book #4)
FACE OF FURY (Book #5)
FACE OF DARKNESS (Book #6)

A JESSIE HUNT PSYCHOLOGICAL SUSPENSE SERIES
THE PERFECT WIFE (Book #1)
THE PERFECT BLOCK (Book #2)
THE PERFECT HOUSE (Book #3)
THE PERFECT SMILE (Book #4)
THE PERFECT LIE (Book #5)

THE PERFECT LOOK (Book #6)
THE PERFECT AFFAIR (Book #7)
THE PERFECT ALIBI (Book #8)
THE PERFECT NEIGHBOR (Book #9)
THE PERFECT DISGUISE (Book #10)
THE PERFECT SECRET (Book #11)
THE PERFECT FAÇADE (Book #12)
THE PERFECT IMPRESSION (Book #13)
THE PERFECT DECEIT (Book #14)
THE PERFECT MISTRESS (Book #15)
THE PERFECT IMAGE (Book #16)
THE PERFECT VEIL (Book #17)
THE PERFECT INDISCRETION (Book #18)
THE PERFECT RUMOR (Book #19)
THE PERFECT COUPLE (Book #20)
THE PERFECT MURDER (Book #21)
THE PERFECT HUSBAND (Book #22)
THE PERFECT SCANDAL (Book #23)
THE PERFECT MASK (Book #24)
THE PERFECT RUSE (Book #25)
THE PERFECT VENEER (Book #26)

CHLOE FINE PSYCHOLOGICAL SUSPENSE SERIES

NEXT DOOR (Book #1)
A NEIGHBOR'S LIE (Book #2)
CUL DE SAC (Book #3)
SILENT NEIGHBOR (Book #4)
HOMECOMING (Book #5)
TINTED WINDOWS (Book #6)

KATE WISE MYSTERY SERIES

IF SHE KNEW (Book #1)
IF SHE SAW (Book #2)
IF SHE RAN (Book #3)
IF SHE HID (Book #4)
IF SHE FLED (Book #5)
IF SHE FEARED (Book #6)
IF SHE HEARD (Book #7)

THE MAKING OF RILEY PAIGE SERIES

WATCHING (Book #1)
WAITING (Book #2)
LURING (Book #3)
TAKING (Book #4)
STALKING (Book #5)
KILLING (Book #6)

RILEY PAIGE MYSTERY SERIES
ONCE GONE (Book #1)
ONCE TAKEN (Book #2)
ONCE CRAVED (Book #3)
ONCE LURED (Book #4)
ONCE HUNTED (Book #5)
ONCE PINED (Book #6)
ONCE FORSAKEN (Book #7)
ONCE COLD (Book #8)
ONCE STALKED (Book #9)
ONCE LOST (Book #10)
ONCE BURIED (Book #11)
ONCE BOUND (Book #12)
ONCE TRAPPED (Book #13)
ONCE DORMANT (Book #14)
ONCE SHUNNED (Book #15)
ONCE MISSED (Book #16)
ONCE CHOSEN (Book #17)

MACKENZIE WHITE MYSTERY SERIES
BEFORE HE KILLS (Book #1)
BEFORE HE SEES (Book #2)
BEFORE HE COVETS (Book #3)
BEFORE HE TAKES (Book #4)
BEFORE HE NEEDS (Book #5)
BEFORE HE FEELS (Book #6)
BEFORE HE SINS (Book #7)
BEFORE HE HUNTS (Book #8)
BEFORE HE PREYS (Book #9)
BEFORE HE LONGS (Book #10)
BEFORE HE LAPSES (Book #11)
BEFORE HE ENVIES (Book #12)
BEFORE HE STALKS (Book #13)

BEFORE HE HARMS (Book #14)

AVERY BLACK MYSTERY SERIES

CAUSE TO KILL (Book #1)
CAUSE TO RUN (Book #2)
CAUSE TO HIDE (Book #3)
CAUSE TO FEAR (Book #4)
CAUSE TO SAVE (Book #5)
CAUSE TO DREAD (Book #6)

KERI LOCKE MYSTERY SERIES

A TRACE OF DEATH (Book #1)
A TRACE OF MURDER (Book #2)
A TRACE OF VICE (Book #3)
A TRACE OF CRIME (Book #4)
A TRACE OF HOPE (Book #5)

Made in United States
North Haven, CT
18 February 2023

32822470R00100